TELLURIA

Jodi Trask

ISBN: 978-1-7751671-1-2

For Jeremy

CHAPTER ONE

Homecoming

The marketplace was a droning nest amid the stacked decrepit Toronto skyline where the only real colour was the New Atlantis projections splashed against the shattered glass towers. It was going to be impossible to find chocolate. I was perhaps among the wealthier clientele of the marketplace that morning, what this a backpack weighed down by five potatoes, thirteen cherry tomatoes, and three apples. The marketplace was a pavilion of booths and tents set up on the cracked pavement along the banks of Lake Ontario. Someone could spend a month there and not see everything. The wares were always changing and the most valuable items you had to ask around for.

It took every ounce of my will not to hug my backpack tight to my chest. Fresh produce was rare and strictly controlled. You were permitted to grow your own if you could, but few people had the knowledge or space. People have been mugged for less. It was safer to act as if you had nothing of any real value and blend into the churning crowd.

I was lucky. It only took an hour to find a couple dealing candy at the centre of the tent city. Most of what they had to sell I'm not sure I would ever risk eating. There were old lemon candies, probably stolen from some abandoned old folks home. The dust was still clinging to the creases of the twisted wrapper. There were fruit gummies in faded packaging that let me know the product would break my teeth off. But right in the middle of the table, half hid under a string of brittle liquorice and a pack of foil wrapped gum were two lonely squares of bakers chocolate.

I waved the woman over to the side of the booth, "Five tomatoes for the chocolate," I offered, speaking just low enough to drown our conversation under the constant drone.

"Ten and something else," The trader replied, looking me over for something of worth. Her eyes fell on my left wrist, "That's a pretty thing."

It was my bracelet - blue and green threads knotted together in a pattern of chevrons, "That's not for trade," I moved my wrist out of her sight. "Nine and an apple."

The trader shrugged, "Ten and two," and put out her hand.

I made the point of muttering under my breath that this was highway robbery as we made the exchange. I took off my backpack and unzipped it just enough to slide my hand in. I fished out the ten tomatoes and the two apples and put the chocolate in the pocket of my battered jacket where they would be safest. The chocolate would be bitter, but we had wild honey at home to sweeten it.

I slipped back into the crowd. There was nothing left for me to do here and I had to hurry home. Outside of the pressing closeness of bodies, I looked up at the nearest projection for the time. I had two hours until Grey came home. If I hurried, there would be plenty of time.

#

The world crumbled in two waves. First, the oil ran out and industry was thrown into chaos. Deliveries halted. In the cities, people were starving. Second, Telluria came. Telluria is a disease that causes it's victim to decompose into one of the four elements; earth, air, fire, or water. Like wildfire, fear spread as fast as the sickness. Anarchy reigned from the desperate need to survive. Families were torn asunder. There was no immunity. There was no cure.

Grey didn't get sick in the first wave of Telluria. Close as siblings, we had each other as his father and my parents fell victim to the disease. New Atlantis developed the cure just in time to save my parents, but not soon enough for Grey's father. I was there when Mr McNair took his last breaths. He had been so pale and insubstantial, little more than a human-shaped cloud laid upon the bed. When he let out his last breath, he faded away like mist at sunrise. Only the faintest breeze remained in the room to remind us that he had been there at all.

When Grey showed the first signs of Telluria - spidery lines like quartz across his shoulder - we were all afraid. His mother especially, after already losing her husband. The day New Atlantis came for him, Grey put up a good show. He hugged his mother and kissed her cheek. "I'll be alright Mom. I'll be back in a week, good as new."

Mrs McNair smiled back, doing her best to be strong for her son, "I know sweetheart. You're in good hands."

He turned to me next and hugged me too. "Take care of them, Terra," he whispered before pressing something into my hand. It was a bracelet made of blue and green threads, knotted together in a chevron pattern.

"Until you come back," I promised and slipped on the bracelet. I glanced over my shoulder at my parents and his mother. Mrs McNair had her hands clasped together so tightly the knuckles were white and she wore a strained smile. My parents, however, were calm, happy even. They wore matching proud smiles. That was some relief. They had the procedure after all. If they weren't worried, was there anything to be worried about?

Grey made an affirmative sound in the back of his throat. Without further goodbyes, he turned and climbed into the New Atlantis ambulance. I stood on the sidewalk as the ambulance drove away, holding back my tears until it was well out of sight.

#

Grey would be home today. His welcome home gift felt like two bars of gold in my pocket. The chocolate probably was just as valuable. Growing up, his favourite treat was always chocolate chip cookies. From the day I found out he would be leaving for treatment, I started saving bits of flour, sugar, and whatever other ingredients that could be spared from the ration deliveries. Chocolate was the only thing that you would never find in the rations. At best, New Atlantis might manage a tiny square as a Christmas treat. But I didn't have that long. My parents

3

weren't even sure I would manage to find it in the marketplace. Mom was prepared to make honey cakes if I failed.

I was filled with an odd mixture of pride and weariness. While I found the chocolate, I still had to get it home. We lived far outside of the urban centre, but thankfully New Atlantis had implemented a fleet of buses retrofitted to run on Essence in most cities. As I waited for my bus, I kept my bag crumpled in my hand as if it were empty. I kept my head down and my body small to be as unassuming as possible. I looked up only when I heard the crunch and pop of tires over a rough road. Mom and Dad used to tell me about the wall-to-wall traffic that plagued the city in the time before. It was hard to imagine now, as the bus bumped along the empty cracked streets. There were a few rusted relics littering the sides of the highway but soon they would be gone like the rest, recycled by New Atlantis and put to better use.

The bus dropped me off about a block away from my house. I ran the rest of the way, leaping over the gravel filled potholes. All of the houses out here looked generally the same. They were all two-story detached homes with peeling paint and falling fences. Mine was no different, neither was Grey's. Both of our yards were converted into gardens rather than all the useless grass. To avoid being raided, it was mostly herbs and useful flowers in the front yards, planted in such a haphazard way that it looked more like wild overgrowth then a garden. The vegetable gardens were in the backyards where they could be protected by a fence. Our houses also bordered an old nature preserve. The forest provided an excellent source of food, which was how we survived fairly well before New Atlantis started passing out rations.

"Mom!" I ran into the house. I found my mother in the kitchen, her hands still caked in rich earth. She must have just come inside from the garden. "Mom I got it!"

Elation chased the confusion on her face, "You didn't! Oh, Terra, that's wonderful! Was it very much?"

"Only ten tomatoes and two apples. A steal. Can we make them now?" I peered out the window as if Grey would be rolling up the street any second. "He's supposed to be back soon isn't he?"

Mom turned the water on in the sink and started scrubbing the dirt from her hands, "Not to worry, we have time. Hurry now, get the flour."

We wouldn't be able to make much. From the careful rationing over the last week, we had enough for a small dozen. But it would be enough. I fetched the other ingredients from the pantry and laid them all out on the counter before taking the chocolate and handing to her directly. "I'll leave it in your hands." We didn't have enough to make a second batch if I messed it up, so I started on supper instead. We would all be having supper together. All of us being me, my parents, Grey and Mrs McNair. It was just a small celebration to have him home.

I took the potatoes from my bag, chopped them into small cubes and put them on to boil. Mrs McNair promised she had a little butter saved, enough for us to make mashed potatoes. We also had fish, which I fried with onion, garlic, and rosemary.

Mom was working the real magic though. With her careful preparations the house soon filled with the smell of fresh cookies. She took them out of the oven just before they were fully cooked, leaving them soft and gooey on the inside.

The meal was almost ready when my father came home. He was coated in a layer of sweat and dust from working in the city greenhouses. In order to qualify for ration deliveries, someone in your home had to work for New Atlantis. Dad was a botanist in the time before, and he made sure the greenhouses were working as efficiently as possible. Mom had a job In the ration warehouse, but she had taken the day off to help me. While I could take junior work positions, New Atlantis encouraged young adults to focus on education instead. They liked to insist we were the future.

While Dad went upstairs to clean up, Mom and I packed up supper to bring next door. While we waited for Dad, I kept looking at the clock. A half hour until he came home, twenty minutes, fifteen. With five minutes to spare we were crossing the yard to the McNair home.

Mrs McNair was sitting on her porch in an old rocking chair. She got up when she saw us and opened her arms to me, "So good of you to come. Grey will be so pleased and- Oh! What do we have here?" She peered into the dish of cookies I was carrying. "My word Terra sweetheart. How on earth did you manage?"

I grinned, feeling rather victorious, "Luck mostly. Mom baked them though."

Mrs McNair chuckled as she released me, "Well, as I recall, last time you baked anything, you made a brick that you called bread." She opened the door and held it open for us, "Hurry now. Just set it on the table. Grey will be here any second."

Inside the table was set. Mrs McNair, who had worked in hospitality in the time before, had gone all out. Her scrubbed wooden table was dressed with a pristine white tablecloth, gleaming silver cutlery, and an antique set of floral china that had belonged to her grandmother. The china and silver I knew were usually hidden under the stairs behind boxes of dusty Christmas decorations. She had roasted a medley of vegetables and baked an aromatic braided bread. We placed our dishes around it and went back outside.

I held Mrs McNair's hand as we waited. She jumped when the clock inside rang the hour. "They were supposed to be here. Terra dear can you see a van coming yet?"

I stepped down onto the driveway and walked out to the sidewalk. "Not yet. But I'm sure it won't be long." I thought of suggesting a cup of tea, but I knew Mrs McNair wasn't going to go inside until her son was here. I walked back towards the step.

"I hope his scar won't be too bad. Such a horrible thing to have to carry with you." Mrs McNair said with a sigh, "He won't mind it of course. Lord knows he'll think it dashing."

I shook my head and stood on the bottom step of the porch, "I'm sure it won't be too bad. Look at Dad's." Dad had the water strain of Telluria. In the days before the cure, his skin had turned transparent and started to drop off him like water. After the cure, all that remained was a small patch the side of his right knee. It was just big enough to see the ghost of his kneecap, but that was all. Mom's scar was a little worse.

She had the fire strain and it left a charred black spot on the back of her neck. When she was sick, it looked like fire burning just below her skin.

Our conversation ceased the moment we heard the soft hiss of an Essence engine. A retrofitted ambulance in the blue and yellow of New Atlantis navigated the many potholes on our street and turned into the McNair driveway. My parents stayed on the porch while Mrs McNair and I walked up to the ambulance. I wondered which of us was more excited, or nervous. The driver stepped out with a clipboard in hand, "I have a Grey McNair. Are you his family?"

"I'm his mother," Mrs McNair answered, eyes darting towards the back of the ambulance.

The driver handed her the clipboard for her to sign the release form. "Right this way," He said after she handed it back.

He made his way towards the back of the ambulance and swung open the patient doors. A stocky boy hopped out. Grey was clad in the same dark t-shirt that might have once been black and faded jeans that he was wearing when he left. He had dark hair and sharp grey eyes that made him look older than our seventeen years.

Mrs McNair ran up and enveloped her son in a bone-crushing hug. He was a little stiff at first, but eventually softened and hugged her back, "Hey, Mom. I'm okay."

Mrs McNair released him and put a hand on either side of his face. Her eyes were sparkling, "My sweet boy. It's so good to have you home." She kissed his cheeks then stepped away to have a quick word with the driver. I spotted her discreetly dab the corners of her eyes with the edge of her sleeve.

"Good to see you're still causing trouble."

I looked to Grey and turned to hug him. Much like with his mother, he was stiff at first but then softened. "Whatever do you mean?" I asked, feigning innocence.

"You just have that look. Like you were up to something." After a delayed second, Grey smiled. It was warm and familiar, but the delay made it feel a little forced. Well, I suppose he did just get out of treatment after all.

I laced my hands behind my back with a grin, "I have a surprise for you."

"Oh?" He raised a singular dark eyebrow.

"You'll see."

Back inside we settled in for a feast. While we ate, Grey told us about his week in treatment. "I can't really remember much of it. Just going to sleep, and a few days later I woke up and was moved to recovery. I slept mostly. I was so tired..." He stopped and waved his hand, "Recovery was alright. I played checkers with this other patient mostly. He said he came from Muskoka and New Atlantis sent an air transport for him rather than attempt the roads."

My eyes flicked to his shoulder. The t-shirt was covering whatever scar he might have left, "But what do they do? How do they cure it?"

He shook his head, "I...Like I said I just kinda went to sleep."

"It was the same for us Terra honey. We told you this." My father chastised gently. They had a nearly identical experience. Both described just falling asleep and then spending the remaining days in sleepy recovery.

Mrs McNair was pouring herself a cup of tea, "All that matters is that it's over and you're home." She smiled at her son. She was doing that a lot during supper, relief and ease flooding her face with every glance.

I shrunk down in my seat a little. I wanted to know more, but people didn't really talk about the cure. I didn't know why. Grey would probably tell me later through when all the parents weren't around.

We finished supper and the cookies came out to the general applause of everyone. Everyone had one, to begin with. They were still

8

warm and the middle was still soft. They were better then I imagined they would be when I set out that morning for the chocolate. Afterwards, the parents sent me and Grey off with the rest of the cookies so that they could clean up

We escaped to the back porch. While it was still light out, the sky was just beginning to take on the red-orange glow of evening. "Terra I can't believe you managed to find chocolate." Grey was just finishing his second cooking, savouring every crumb.

I laughed, "It was nothing. I think people are getting worse at bartering. They practically gave it away."

"Or they just met a formidable opponent? I didn't think people even made chocolate anymore." Last time either of us had chocolate was probably ten years ago or more. Before Telluria went rampant. Before New Atlantis. At the twilight time between what the world was and what the world became.

"Grey..." I looked over my shoulder at the window, just to be sure that it wasn't open. "Won't you tell me now? What it was like?"

Grey froze. His face turned blank and twitched like a machina rebooting. His familiar smile quickly replaced it, "You've heard about it from your parents."

I bit my lip, frustrated between wanting to know and wanting to give him his space. But this was Grey. "But...other sick people were there. Did you see anyone far along?"

"A few." Grey's expression darkened. "I really don't want to talk about it yet Terra. I just got out remember?"

Grey used to be just as curious as I was. I was hoping that he would come back full of stories. But, I had to admit it made a certain kind of sense that he wouldn't want to talk about it. I sighed and looked up at the darkening sky, "So you're okay now? It's all gone?"

"It's never all gone." He pointed out, "But yeah."

"Is it scarred much?" I didn't dare ask at the supper table. I pushed the topic too far at the time as it was. Plus it probably would have upset Mrs McNair.

Silently, Grey pulled up the sleeve of his shirt. A thin tracery of pale lines was etched into his skin. "That's most of it. It wraps around to my shoulder blade a little, but at least it won't spread now."

My breath came in sharp. It was bigger then I remembered. How much did it grow just during his treatment? "Does it hurt?"

Grey pulled his sleeve back down. "Not anymore. I don't feel...anything now. Nothing."

There was a strange tone in his voice that I couldn't quite place. "What about the cure? Did it-"

He shook his head before I even finished the question, "I didn't feel anything. Like I said, I was asleep." In a sudden reappearance of his old self, Grey flashed a grin and messed up my unruly dark curls. "Stop worrying about it. Nothing's going to change. I'm back now and it'll be the same as it always has been."

CHAPTER TWO

The Truth That Binds Us

I assumed that Grey and I would fall back into our own habits. Before he left, we were inseparable. We would always take the same junior work positions. We always went to the market together. When Dad sent me into the woods for wild mushrooms or honey, I could usually count of Grey to come along. Things seemed easier when we were together. We had an unspoken language, we made a good team.

I should have expected that things would be different when he got back. Telluria had that effect on people. When they left for treatment, they never came back quite the same. It was never that something was wrong exactly, just different. New Atlantis explained it away as the normal response to a traumatizing event. For years Telluria was a death sentence. The cure was still so young that the fear and stigma of the disease was carried in everyone's hearts.

I first encountered this change in my own parents. They came back from treatment as the same people, but something was just slightly...off. Mom stopped listening to the old records she adored. Dad didn't laugh as much. It was the same for Grey. Grey was just a little too serious. He was just a little too dedicated to paying back New Atlantis for curing him. I understood, I really did. I was just waiting for the day when I would stop noticing the subtle differences between my Grey, and this new one.

It was three days before I was able to talk to him properly. He took a permanent job with New Atlantis that kept him busy throughout the day. At night he buried himself in his studies. New Atlantis (and our parents) encouraged young people to strive for an education, we would be the ones rebuilding this world. But still, I missed him. I wanted my friend back.

Wednesday was cloudy but nice. I spent most of the day in the woods behind our house. It was late summer, but I had already started building up our winter stores. My father taught me just about every edible plant that could be found in our woods. Those woods kept our two families alive before New Atlantis.

I returned mid-afternoon with my backpack bursting with herbs and berries. I stopped in the shed to bundle and hang the herbs to dry. Inside the house, I washed the berries and put them on the stove to cook down into jam. It was mostly blueberries. Maybe if we started saving up flour rations now, we could have blueberry pie for Thanksgiving.

Once the jam was done, I set it aside to cool. With nothing else to do, I fetched the battered calculus book with a shiny "New Atlantis" stamp on the front cover from my room and went to the front porch.

I was midway through some practice questions when I heard the crunch of gravel. I looked up and I saw that Grey was just coming home.

"Grey!" I dropped my book on the front step and ran across our yards.

He was nearly at the door and had the look of a startled bunny. "Oh. Hey, Terra."

"I found some wild blueberries," I blurted, trying to stop him from locking himself inside again. "I made jam and we'll probably have some tonight with supper. You should come."

I was expecting something in the range of delight but his face barely rippled from blank passivity. "I'm behind in my studies."

I stood up a little straighter. "Oh good! I was just working on some calculus, come quiz me." I reached for his arm, meaning to tug him along to my front porch but it was like holding a rock.

12

"No."

I let go and tried not to feel the defeat pressing on my shoulders. "Oh... well... I mean it doesn't need to be calculus. I'm disastrously behind in history, or-"

"I would prefer to work alone Terra."

My breath caught and I tried not to feel wounded by his sudden snap. "But-"

"I-" There was a flicker of something, just behind his eyes. Almost like a flinch but not quite. He smiled. It was the warm Grey half smile that I'd seen a million times before. "No sorry. I'm just... really busy. I'm so behind and I've been trying to help Mom. It's just her and-" he sighed as he ran a hand through his hair, "How about a sleepover? Tomorrow night? Like old times."

It was like watching a subtle Jekyll and Hyde. I raised one incredulous eyebrow. "Just like old times? You won't snap at me again?"

Rather than defending himself he just looked confused at that statement. "Uh... sure? I'll even pile all the blankets in the den and you bring some jam. If there's any left. I'll even let you pick the movie."

I had no idea what was going on but I would accept it. At least he was starting to act a little more like himself. I managed a half-smile of my own. "Oooooh, you are going to regret that offer, McNair. You have a deal."

#

There are seven things that you need for a proper Grey-Terra sleepover; clothes, toothbrush, hairbrush, flashlights, movies, food and duct tape. Why duct tape? Because it's damn useful and that is all that need be said on the subject.

Six of the seven were packed in my backpack, which was sitting on the front porch. Food took some planning. There was the jam (obviously) and Grey was supplying bread. There was also one solitary cookie, a couple apples and - after walking around the edge of the woods for a little while - I found wild hazelnuts.

The sun was setting, and the sky was on fire when I crossed the yards and to Grey's house. Grey and his mother were both in the kitchen, cleaning up from their own supper. "Oh, Terra dear. Good, you can help put these away." Mrs McNair handed me a pile of clean dishes. She looked exhausted. There were dark circles under her eyes.

"Are you alright Mrs McNair?"

"Oh certainly. It's been a long week."

"Are you sure there's no way I can help?" I asked. I didn't usually work, so maybe I could help her around the house or something.

"You are too sweet. But we'll manage," she patted my cheek and crossed the room. "I'll be right next door if either of you needs me, okay?" She kissed both Grey's cheeks first and then did the same to me. "Your parents were kind enough to invite me over. You two have fun."

"Sure Mom. Have fun!" Grey said with a wave as she slipped out the front door.

"What are they doing?" I asked once she was gone.

He gave a small shrug. "Something about your father's rhubarb wine being ready," I gagged and Grey laughed. "Oh come on. It wasn't that bad."

"Speak for yourself." Once, a few years ago, we had gotten into Dad's homemade wine. My parents thought that the splitting headache and nausea the next day were punishment enough.

We went downstairs into the den. The den was Grey's self-appointed man cave. The rest of the house was very much his mothers. All ancient doilies and little pretty odds and ends but this part of the house was Grey's. A dull brown sectional was squeezed into a corner. A screen and disc player sat lovingly on a pedestal of Grey's old toy box. As promised, in the very centre of the room was a pile of probably every blanket and pillow in the house. Including the quilt off Grey's own bed and throw pillows from the living room.

Grey grabbed my hand and pulled me into the blanket nest. "So what movies did you decide to torture me with?" He asked, flicking

14

on the TV. The New Atlantis Broadcasting Channel flickered to life, the only channel.

"Disney. Sappy romances. All your favourites,"

"I take it no Sixth Sense?" He asked with a pout.

"You've watched that a thousand times!" Perhaps literally.

"But that ending!" He threw his hands up like a teacher giving up on a student. "Fine... mm... 'Beauty and the Beast'?"

I peered up at him through my lashes. "You decided quickly for a man about to be 'tortured' McNair."

He slumped back against the seat of the couch. "What can I say? I'm a fan of the singing candelabra."

#

I didn't remember falling asleep. I remembered a dancing dish rendition of 'Be Our Guest', AKA Grey's favourite part. Then a pillow collided with my face.

"Better wake up before I eat your share of the jam." He was sitting in the middle of the nest, a piece of toast with jam balanced between his hands. On the TV the evening news was on, the volume turned down low.

I sat up slowly, shivering. Was it this cold earlier? I dug my way further under the nest of blankets and took the offered piece of toast. "Did you actually watch it all after I fell asleep? What time is it?"

"Yes, and eleven o'clock," he gestured to a bowl next to him, "I cut up the apples you brought too."

We feasted on the toast and apples and split the single cookie, feeling much like kings. I wondered if this was how New Atlantis higher ups ate every day. On the TV, the image flickered to a riot outside of a New Atlantis building. On one side, sign-wielding citizens were shouting something. They were too far from the microphone to be heard properly. On the other, New Atlantis Guards stood impenetrable in machina suits. Curious, I turned up the volume.

"Protesters were outside a New Atlantis facility in Seattle, Washington today. Reports say the protesters voiced opinions about the use of the Telluria treatment, citing that New Atlantis officials have not disclosed the full side effects. New Atlantis President Nikolai Wolfe released a statement saying that the cure was perfectly safe and only caused minor fatigue for 2-4 days after administration. Protesting groups such as these have been reported outside New Atlantis buildings worldwide. As of yet all reports indicate that protests have remained peaceful, but the increase in volume-"

The screen when black. Beside me, Grey was holding the remote. His face was contorted with rage, his body was tight as a bow about to fire. "Grey, what's wrong?"

"Them. Those worthless sacks of shit," he hissed, pointing at the TV. "You know I saw them when I went for treatment. They were outside with their signs and their shouts."

"The protestors?" I looked from the blank TV to him. Last time I saw him this angry someone had attacked his mother in the street. "You can't be serious Grey. They are just more of those idiots who don't trust modern medicine. It's the same as those anti-vax moms from when we were kids. We laugh at them remember. Come on Grey, it's not like they can do anything to stop it."

"That's not the point Terra. These are the kind of people who would see the cure taken away." A growl ripped from his throat and he turned to look me dead in the eye. "Don't you understand! If they had their way I would have died! Your parents would have died! Honestly, Terra, I thought you were smarter than this."

That shouldn't have stung as much as it did, but I felt tears welling in my eyes. "You don't think I remember what it was like to watch Mom's fever get so high that her eyes were literally glowing with the heat inside her? You don't think I remember my Dad melting? Melting, Grey. You don't think I remember you-" I wiped at the tears, determined not to let him talk to me this way. I wasn't a child who didn't know better just because he was sick and I wasn't. "You don't need to slap me in the face with it Grey. Jeez, calm the hell down. It's just silly protesters. They can't stop the cure."

16

Grey opened his mouth to start a reply and then stopped. The fury drained from his face. He looked almost confused. He blinked, and his body relaxed. He slumped back down in the nest of blankets. "Sorry. I overreacted. Your right, they can't stop it." While he had calmed down in an unexplainable number of seconds, I could still hear the venom in his tone.

I could only assume he overreacted because of what he had just been through. But still, it was so unlike Grey to fly off the handle like that, then to calm down just as quickly. He was acting like a flash flood, miles from the calm and sensible demeanour I always knew.

Grey reached over and picked another movie from the pile. 'Frozen'. One of my favourites and I suspected he picked it just to placate me. Still bitter, I pulled blankets up on the couch with me and settled in for the movie.

Even under the blankets, I shivered, why was it so unnaturally cold down here? Grey didn't seem to notice the cold at all. Under the blankets, I was so snug and warm that I was asleep again before 'Let it Go'.

#

For the second time, Grey was shaking me awake. The TV was splashed with white noise. Grey was sitting on the floor next to where I was sleeping moments before. I was lying on my stomach, my left arm hanging out of the blankets off the side of the couch. "Mmm...what is it now Grey? What time is it?" I murmured. It was near midnight last time I checked.

"You need to leave," his voice was tight. "You need to leave now."

I sat up, an uncomfortable beat stirring in my chest. "Why?"

"Hurry up. Get dressed. You need to be gone before they get here," he tossed my backpack at me.

"Grey what's going on?! I'm not doing anything until you tell me why you are kicking me out at-" I finally spotted the tv remote and switched on the NABC. It was 4:24. "I am not going out at 4 in the

17

blessed morning! Whatever you're on about can wait until at least sunrise." I threw a pillow at him and pulled the blankets over me again. At least, it wasn't cold anymore. I felt heavy with sleep. My eyes drooping before I even reached the pillow.

Grey grabbed my left arm and twisted it. "Look!" He commanded, holding my left wrist towards my face. Along my forearm, thin grey lines stretched out across my skin like quartz veins. Exactly like quartz veins.

"N-no. No!" I tasted bile in my throat. "N-no I can't. I can't!" I yanked my arm away and rubbed the lines with my thumb. They were sharp and gritty and they weren't coming off.

"You have it, Terra," Grey whispered. He touched his own shoulder where I knew matching scars laid just under his shirt. "You'll be Earth-type then... like me."

"B-but..." I swallowed hard. With clumsy fingers, I pulled a warm sweater over my t-shirt. "I need to go to the clinic. I need to-"

Grey grabbed me again. He yanked me close by the next of my sweater and made me meet his eyes. "They are already coming. I had to call them. I saw it... I had to. I'm sorry. I'm sorry. I can't stop it." He pushed me away and handed me my backpack. For just a second there was a flicker of tenderness in the wild gleam of his eyes. "I had to call them understand. I couldn't help it. I had to."

I slipped my arms through the straps of my bag. My head bobbed in a small nod. "I... I know... it could kill me. I need to go..."

"NO!" Grey's rejection was so sudden that I jumped. "You can't go with them! Don't get the cure! D-don't Terra!" Grey winced as if it hurt to say no. He took my wrist and pulled me up the stairs. "They'll be here soon. You have to run. Get out of town. Keep it covered. For the love of God Terra don't let them get you. They'll be here soon. I'm sorry. I'm so sorry. I had to call them. I had no choice. I... I had to."

I was trembling once we made it to the kitchen. Grey let go of me and was pulling food from the cupboards. He reached for my bag and started dropping in whatever he could.

18

"Grey stop! STOP!" I screamed. "I don't understand. I have to get it. If I don't..." Tears started to sting my eyes. The image of my parents on the verge of death danced behind my eyelids. "I have to. I d-don't want to die Grey. I have to."

His eyes were frantic. The grey irises he was named for were flecked with dancing gold in the pale moonlight streaming through the back window. "D-don't. Worse...worse than death. It breaks you...it breaks..." Grey hissed sharply and his hand flew to the back of his neck. He stumbled and I held on to steady him.

"Grey... Grey, you're not making sense. You said the cure was good. You had it yourself and you're fine. Grey please!"

His smile was weak, the pain was shining in his eyes. "They make me say it's good. They make your parents say it. They make everyone-" Another sharp hiss and Grey tumbled to the ground. I was pulled down with him. "They take the illness. They don't cure it. It's not a cure...it hurts..."

It was the sound of tires and engines that made us both look up. Lights streamed across the house from the front window. Grey pulled himself up by the counter, wincing from a pain that I could not see. He took my wrist and pulled me towards the door. "Run. Don't get caught. Don't trust New Atlantis. Don't trust the cured. Show no one..."

They were knocking on the door. Polite at first, but it was getting more insistent. We could hear them calling out. Grey braced against the counter and pushed me towards the back door. "Run," he hissed and crushed his lips against mine. He tasted of salt and sweat. I could smell his sharp soap. He never kissed me before. Ever. My heart clenched amid the staccato beats.

The door broke open. He pushed me away. I stumbled out the back door just as the kitchen was swarmed.

"Run Terra! Run!" Grey screamed.

The New Atlantis officers surrounded him. They pulled his arms behind his back. Others were advancing on me. I turned and ran through the back door. I just needed to get as far as the woods. There I could hide.

I scurried up the fence, muscle memory alone guiding my feet to the right footholds. Officers were running across the yard after me. At the top of the fence, I looked back. They had Grey on his knees on the kitchen floor, his arms still held behind him in a way that suggested shackles. "RUN! RUN! TERRA RUN! RU-" There was the flash of cold steel. The explosion of a bullet. Grey's screams were silenced.

CHAPTER THREE

Alone

I sprinted into the woods amid a cacophony of shouts and gunshots. In the darkness, I stumbled over branches and rocks. My palms were bleeding. I didn't dare stop to find my flashlight. I knew these woods. I kept running hoping that I could lose them in the dark.

Over the fallen tree trunk. Down the three-foot drop. A sharp turn to the east. I didn't have a plan. I couldn't think. I couldn't breathe. My body was moving, I was following. Around a rock. Across a stream. The voices became steadily fainter behind me. I needed a place to hide. Where? I didn't know of any caves in these woods. Not even so much as a hollow beneath the tree roots. I had nowhere to go.

I came to another stream and followed it. Just in case they had search dogs, I walked through the water to lose my scent. It wouldn't come to that, would it? How desperate would they be to find a dying girl?

With the freezing cold water slapping around my ankles and the last of distant shouts dying away, I started to think again. They had killed Grey. From there... I didn't understand anything with absolute certainty. Grey had said that he had to call them, and yet he told me not to go with them. Why would he report me, then aid in my escape? I pulled on the sleeve of my sweater, not wanting to see the lines on my wrist even by accident. How long did I have? Some people lived years after the mark appeared. Others, weeks. Wouldn't it be faster to just let the New Atlantis officers come shoot me? I shook that idea off as quickly as it came. Grey did not give his life for me to give up on mine. I had to keep going, I had to. For just a little longer.

There was still the matter of shelter. The sky was already starting to lighten. While the streaks of gold and rose weren't yet on the horizon, it would only be another hour or so and I had nowhere to hide for the day.

I followed the stream a little further. I knew there was a small pool nearby with fish and clean water. It would be a good place to hide until I had a better plan.

The clawing woods opened up into a small clearing, just big enough for the pool and a bit of land around it. I stepped onto the banks and sank to my knees. The surge of adrenaline that had brought me this far was almost depleted and fresh tears were clinging to my lashes. I just need a place to hide. Anywhere...just for today.

The air filled with the rumble and crash of shifting rocks. Across the pool, shrouded by near dawn mist, I saw a jutting precipice of stone break through the mossy damp ground.

With everything else that had already happened tonight, I couldn't bring myself to a reaction. The mass of stone looked as though it had always been a part of the landscape. It was covered in a convincing layer of fine moss and tiny weeds clinging to the cracks. Some part of my exhausted mind just wanted to believe that it was always there.

I got up and walked along the pool's shore to the new formation. Facing the water, there was a crevice in the base of the rock just large enough for me to squeeze through. The opening was partially hidden by a small berry bush. Setting down my backpack, I knelt down and climbed into the little cave. The inside had a low ceiling just high enough so I was able to comfortably sit up. It was deep enough for me to lie down with a little wiggle room all around. I could hide here, at least for the night. I curled up on the earthen floor with my bag as a pillow. Hidden for the moment and finally safe, everything that had happened crashed down on me. I buried my face in my hands, stifling the wracking sobs that shook through my body. My best friend was dead. My best friend was killed by an organization we all had been taught to trust and respect. Every rustle of leaves and every snapping twig sounded like a gun. I tried to cover my ears, but nothing blocked out the single gunshot I heard over and over again to the dawn.

#

I stayed in the cave for three days. I had a little food left in my bag and could get water from the pond. I knew I wouldn't be able to stay there forever. Winter was coming and I wasn't prepared for it. Not to mention, it was a miracle that I wasn't already found. I could hear them sometimes. New Atlantis officers tramping through the woods like so many elephants calling out my name. I could hear them saying that they wouldn't hurt me and they just wanted to help. Yeah, like they helped Grey.

On the second day, I heard my parents. I wanted to go to them. I wanted to go to them more than anything. I squeezed my eyes shut and covered my ears until they stopped. They wanted to hand me over to the New Atlantis officers as well. I could hear them say it. Calling out for me. I clutched my bag like it was an anchor and waited for them to give up.

On the third day, I woke only to the sound of rustling leaves and chirping birds. Unless you spent some time in the woods, you wouldn't believe just how loud birds could be first thing in the morning. I took a cautionary look through the bushes before crawling out of my little sanctuary into the streaming dewy sunlight. I would have to leave today. I pulled out my backpack and sat down at the water's edge. I cleaned up as best I could, splashing water in my face and pulling a brush through my hair. I pulled the hood of my sweater up to hide my face. If they were still looking for me... I didn't want to be immediately recognizable.

Without any solid plan, I started south. My dad once told me that you could tell south by the moss on the trees. In lieu of the north star to put my back to it seemed as good a plan as any. I knew there was a small city roughly south of me. Then I would keep going. Keep walking south until I found a nice quiet place to stop and-

I tugged the sleeve of my sweater down a little more. I could live months yet. Hell, I might live years. Or, as I remembered the quick

23

succession of symptoms I saw in my own parents, I might only last weeks. I took one last look at the small cave that had been my home and refuge the past three days. No, I wouldn't just wait to die. As easy as that would be it would be spitting in the face of Grey's memory. My heart clenched like a vice and I started south.

#

Without any real idea of where I was going, major landmarks sort of snuck up on me. That first night I slept in the tall grasses on the side of the highway. By the next afternoon, I arrived in a small city. The sign at the border said, Hamilton. I took the first bus I found. All buses led to a city centre where I could hopefully find a market. I didn't really need food, as I had filled my backpack on the way out of the woods, but it never hurt to see what was available. If nothing, I could take a southbound bus and keep going.

The marketplace was on a patch of roads and bare pavement in front of a large gleaming building. It had to be a New Atlantis building to be in such good condition. Stalls were set up in some semblance of rows. It was not as busy as I was used to, which made me feel enough at ease to keep my hood down, letting the fresh air blow through my hair.

It was all the usual wares; fresh fruits, vegetables, sweets and mini-luxuries that were rare to find in the ration packages. There was a man selling two bicycles. I wouldn't have minded one, but he would likely want everything I owned as payment, including most of the clothes off my back. Pity, it would have made the journey easier. I sighed softly, seeing nothing worth parting with my few belongings. I was preparing to find the buses when I happened to look up at the New Atlantic alerts projected on the side of the gleaming building.

My stomach dropped. An enlarged picture of myself looked back at me. It was the picture from my New Atlantis identification. I read the notice under my picture. 'MISSING. APPROACH WITH CAUTION. UNCURED TELLURIAN. WANTED FOR QUESTIONING ON THE DEATH OF RECENTLY CURED NEIGHBOUR.'

I took a shaky step back. Wanted for questioning? Was New Atlantis really trying to say that I was responsible for Grey's death? Acid flooded my veins. How could they! My parents would never believe this, would they? But then, I remembered how they had called for me in the forest. Their pleading voices saying that New Atlantis just wanted to help me. Would they be so willing to hand me over if they knew what New Atlantis had done?

Turning on the spot, I ran south. As far and fast as possible. The biting, clawing, rise of acid clung to my throat. I wanted to scream. A bus was pulling up to a stop ahead of me. I pulled up my hood and leapt through one of the back open doors. Inside kept my face towards the window. I just needed to get out of here.

The bus brought me to the outskirts of a suburban area. Rows of identical houses all in neatly arranged streets. I got off the bus and started walking. With the initial shock fading, I felt weak and tears stung my eyes.

#

This went on for days, I walked when I had to. Otherwise, I took buses from housing areas to urban centres, then from urban centres to housing areas. Every so often people would look at me strangely and the clawing fear that I was being recognized would rise again. Though as I thought about it during the long bouts of walking, I rationalized that I hadn't showered in days and I was filthy. Homelessness was a thing of the past. If you didn't have a home, New Atlantis provided one, simple as that. There was no reason for someone to look the way I did. I tried to remedy this by splashing water on my face in streams or keeping my hair brushed, but I didn't have soap and, therefore, nothing could be done about the smell. Even on the hottest days, I always kept my sweater on now. The mark on my arm was slowly growing and was threatening to crawl past my wrist.

Maybe it was the dream of a bath or maybe it was just the general heat that led me to Niagara. The distant roar of crushing water beckoned to me like something out of my most dizzying daydreams. I promised myself that I would have a bath there somehow. Screw however contaminated the water probably was.

Once again I took the bus and found the marketplace. Like Toronto, Niagara's market was set on the banks of Lake Ontario. It was a little unnerving to think that if I had the ability to see that far, Toronto's marketplace was just across the water.

I needed soap and I cringed at the idea of how expensive it was going to be. Soap was one of the necessities given by New Atlantis and whatever I found there was going to be artisanal. After an hour-long search, I found a stall with a table covered completely in small soap cakes of pale pink, lavender and yellow. Some of the soap even had dried flowers embedded in them. I looked up at the seller; he was a young man with black hair and eyes the same colour as the crashing falls. "What can you give me for a handful of wild hazelnuts?" I asked.

The boy tilted his head but before he could reply a hush fell over the crowd. A New Atlantis truck pulled up to the market and two officers got out. I simultaneously wanted to run and stay frozen in place. My hood was already up so I tilted my head down to hide my face but I could still see them in the corner of my eye. They were moving through the crowd stopping people at random, ordering to see their hand. An officer held a small device no bigger than then one of the soap cakes and would press it against the offered hand. Every time there was a beep and a small flash of green light. Satisfied, the officers would let the person go before moving on to someone else.

"It's to check your blood you know," the soap seller said. I jumped and looked back up at him. He was following the two officers with his eyes. "With all the racket the resistance has been making lately, a couple days ago New Atlantis announced that officers would be performing random checks. Seems like a waste of time to me. What sane person would hide the fact that they were sick?" He looked back at me. It might have been the sun glaring off the water but I could have sworn he winked.

With the officers so close, running would be impossible. I was already a wanted woman and attracting attention wouldn't help. Hoping to render myself invisible, I pointed at one of the soaps again. "That one for the hazelnuts. Fresh picked just a couple days ago."

"Eh...take it on the house. I dare say you need it. Fell in mud did you?" He made a pointed look towards my wrist where my sleeve was riding up. The edge of my mark was just poking through. My pulse hammered in my neck and I tugged my sleeve down. I had to admit, it did sort of look like caked on mud. He handed me the soap cake and nodded towards the falls. "Best run along sweetheart. That way I think."

I looked where he indicated and saw it led away from the New Atlantis van. Away from the officers in a fairly crowded area where I could get lost in the press of bodies. I slipped the soap in my pocket and started moving at a steady pace through the crowd. I almost thought I had escaped when I felt a hand on my shoulder. I turned and found myself face to face with one of the officers. "Your hand Miss?"

My stomach was full of rocks. I didn't dare look up at him. Rather, I turned and gestured vaguely to the bus stop. "I...I'm in a hurry. My grandmother...it's her birthday and I..." I swallowed hard. "I'm going to miss my bus."

The officer chuckled. "And I suppose the big bad wolf will be waiting if you don't hurry along?" He offered, though not unkindly. "Come now, it's just a little test. Less than a second and you'll be on your way."

He reached for my hand. I was out of options. I pushed the officer hard and ran.

"Stop! I command you to stop!" The officer shouted behind me. I grabbed at people, bikes, anything and pushed them into my pursuer's path. My feet pounded against the paving stones, I ducked into an alley, coming out onto the street beyond. A bus honked and careened around me. Officers were shouting behind me, more than one now. I ran across the street and through the next alley, making a sharp turn to the left on the other side. The hum of an engine was behind me. I heard the screech of tires, saw a flash of blue and yellow in my periphery. The van rounded to a stop directly in my path. The side panel slid open, two officers pulled me in, and a sharp prick in my arm led me into blackness.

\#

Most teenagers know the feeling. That pounding drum between your eyes and how every sound is amplified to megaphones. The world just can't seem to stop moving despite the fact that you are 98% sure that you are lying still. I knew the feeling. Some months previous, Grey had found an old dusty bottle of tequila tucked away in the back of a cupboard in his mother's sitting room. I was able to get exactly one lemon from the market, Grey already had the salt.

The gunshot through Grey's head broke up the memory making the tequila daydream fade in the ripples of blood and reality. I groaned and as it all came back in slow progression; the market, the man with the soap, running from the New Atlantis officer, the van. It was the last thing I could remember, that damned blue and yellow van.

I could hear beeping and then the sterile hiss of a door sliding open. I opened my eyes just a crack to see I was in a bed. No, it wasn't quite a bed. More like a partially open tube. Curved stainless steel walls rose around me. I tried to ignore my aching hand and motioned to sit up. Ugh, why couldn't I move?

"Oh not so fast," a cool clinical voice spoke from somewhere in the direction of my feet. It was a woman in a white lab coat and a stethoscope around her neck. "Your chart says you were given quite the dose of sedatives. You'll be dizzy, best stay still."

I tried again to sit up but found myself blocked. Looking down, I saw there was a leather strap across my chest. "Wh-what is this?" I looked up at her. "Where am I?"

"It's just a precaution. As I said, you were sedated and you were bound to be dizzy. It's so you wouldn't fall out of bed."

I looked pointedly at the walls of my bed pod thing. Falling seemed the least of my worries. "Where am I?"

"Not to worry. You are in the St. Catherine's Telluria Treatment Facility. Just lie back and relax. The technician will be in shortly to begin your treatment."

I couldn't breathe. I thrashed in time with the pounding in my head. "N-no! I don't want it! Let me go! I don't want your cure!" I reached for the strap against my chest but I found that my hands were also bound, as were my feet.

The woman smiled coolly. "Of course you want the cure. You don't want to die do you? Just calm down and you'll be released in no time. Your parents are very anxious to get you back."

That brought me up short. "M-my parents?"

"Of course. They are waiting for you at home right now. After your treatment, you'll be sent right back."

In spite of myself, I stopped thrashing. "But... but I saw... the sign. I'm wanted. Grey- "

"Mr McNair's death was an unfortunate accident. It wasn't you that attacked him, Miss Chase, it was your illness. No one blames you for what happened." The woman was standing at my bedside now. She was smiling in that way you might smile at a child. "All that matters now is that you get well and return to your family."

"B-but..." My eyes darted around. This couldn't be real. "It wasn't me! It was... the officers shot him! They shot him because he warned me! Let me go! Let me go!" I strained against the bindings. There was a rumbling in the floor like a small earthquake and then the sound of tiles exploding on my right.

The woman was no longer looking at me. She was transfixed, staring horrified at something on the floor. After two excruciatingly long heartbeats, she dashed around my bed hit a button at the foot of the pod. There was a hiss and a glass panel slip over the front of my pod. I could still see the woman. She retreated to the far wall, still gazing in horror at the floor as she reached for the phone. Her voice was muffled through the glass.

I screamed. The bindings bit into my wrists as I thrashed and pulled with all my strength. How could I possibly get out? I hit something with my left hand and felt a long raking sting. How the hell did that happen? At the moment I didn't care. I raked the leather strap across the stone, slowly cutting away at it until I was able to slip that hand free. I clawed at the strap on my chest. Clumsy, bloody fingers

29

pulled the strap loose, and then the strap on my other hand. I could move a little now, but my feet were still bound. I twisted, reaching down through the pod. There was little room to move. I felt my fingers brush my knee, my shin, inch by inch getting closer to my ankles.

More doctors rushed into the room. They were shouting though nothing made sense to me. I focused on a single task. My fingers brushed a strap and closed over a cold metal clasp.

Several of the doctors were at the foot of the bed now. More buttons were being pressed and the pod was filling with an opaque opal gas that seemed to almost shimmer in the fluorescent light of the room. My left arm suddenly felt like it was on fire. I could feel every line of my mark burning and growing hotter. It felt like the air was running out in the pod. If I could only hold still my treacherous heart and make it let me breathe slower.

I fumbled with the buckle, pulling, and tugging on the strap until it loosened enough for my foot to slip out. I was struggling to concentrate as I twisted to free my other foot. What was this opal gas? I hardly noticed the room around me erupting into chaos.

Another group of people burst in. Not doctors but average people as if they had just charged in off the street. Amid more blurred shouting, I scraped for the second ankle strap. The gas in the chamber was getting thicker. I couldn't see what I was doing anymore and was going by feel alone. I was going to pass out at this rate. Either from the gas or the burning in my arm.

The pod hissed and the glass panel slid back. The opal gas dissipated and I pushed myself up. Even with the gas gone, I felt drunk as I freed my foot and attempted climbing out of the pod. By 'climbing', I really meant something more akin to 'falling'. My legs were jello and someone caught me under the arms so I wouldn't fall.

"Merlin help her to the truck. Carry her if you have to. Kalle, Frank, cover our retreat." The command came from a tall blonde man by the door. The floor was littered with unconscious doctors.

The person named Merlin led me towards the door. I was able to take two steps before my legs collapsed beneath me. What the hell did that opal coloured gas do to me? I looked up at Merlin through half-lidded eyes. He kept a firm grip under my arms, "You," I murmured. Black hair and eyes like a waterfall. I recognized him from somewhere.

"Can you get on my back? Hold on to my neck," I braced against the pod as he let me go and crouched in front of me. "I know you're tired. You can rest soon."

I clambered on his back and looped my arms over his shoulders. I was too dizzy at the time to consider that I might have been stepping out of the frying pan and straight into hellfire. Whatever that opal gas was, it left me feeling drained and my arm was still throbbing. "Wh-where-"

"Shhh. You're going someplace safe. Just hold on." There were two others in front of us, and two behind. I was jostled as they ran in a tight formation down immaculate hallways. The ceiling lights seemed to flash overhead as we ran past them. Just as I was beginning to wonder why no one had raised the alarm, I was bombarded by howling sirens. There were shouts coming from somewhere behind us.

"They caught up fast. Hurry, through the back." The blonde man in front yelled.

"But Josh! That's the essence room. Isn't there-" This time it was a mousy faced girl who was running beside Josh at the front.

"They won't risk shooting in there. It's the safest way. Just don't think about it."

We crashed through a set of double doors into a sterile white space with the hum of fans. The only thing in the room was a row of cabinets and another set of double doors. There was a moment of hesitation among the group before we charged forward.

I lifted my head to see over Merlin's shoulder. It was a warehouse. There were hundreds of pods set in perfect rows. I couldn't see the people inside since every single pod was filled with the opal gas. The gas was being piped in from a network of tubes that crisscrossed the ceiling, an end coming down to each pod. I had the unnerving

31

sensation of being caught in a spider's web. "What is it?" My voice was little more than a croak.

"Essence," Merlin hissed.

Without further explanation, the group started forward at a run. I held on to Merlin's neck as tight as my lead arms would allow. He kept a strong grip on my legs and I hoped it would be enough to keep me from falling.

"Stop!" The shout came from four New Atlantis employees behind us. Thankfully, as Josh guessed, they did not risk to shoot. If it really was essence in those tubes, it was too valuable to risk a leak. Not for one girl.

"Hurry! Through here!" Josh pushed on a door at the end of the warehouse and we poured into another sterile chamber. From there it was another set of double doors, a hall, and suddenly we were running out into the cool evening air.

Tires squealed on the pavement and a blue and yellow van pulled up in front of us. The side panel slid open. "It's about time you got out! Hop in," the driver yelled.

I slid from Merlin's back and he lifted me into the van as everyone else was clambering in. The van door slid shut just as the pursuing officers came bursting out the back doors in our wake.

My entire body lurched at the sound of gunshots. We accelerated towards the facility gate. Roaring engine and squealing tires were met with the sharp ting of at least one bullet hitting the van. Nothing was piercing the metal thank goodness. Why would a New Atlantis van need an armoured shell?

The group erupted into cheers the moment we broke through the gate. There were eight people in total, including me. My heartfelt as though it was pounding in sludge. With flooding relief of escaping that place, my eyes were getting heavy. I tugged on Merlin's arm. "Where..." I repeated again.

He patted my shoulder. "You're safe now. Get some rest. I'll wake you up when we get there. Then you can ask all the questions you want."

Last time I fell unconscious in a blue and yellow van, I woke up in a healing pod. I fought my drooping eyes as long as I could. The others in the van had broken into celebrating conversation, and I was lulled back into black oblivion.

CHAPTER FOUR

Negotiations

"Good morning. Well...evening really."

I jolted awake at the quasi-familiar voice and sat up. Stars immediately formed in my eyes and I had to lie back down to keep the world from spinning. I was lying on a small brass bed in a sterile looking room with white everything except for the robin egg linoleum floor.

"Hey, careful now. You've been asleep nearly twenty-four hours."

I turned my head enough to look towards the voice. Black hair, sea eyes, Merlin was sitting next to my bed in a folding metal chair.

"You."

He grinned, "Yes me. Though hello is generally a more customary greeting," he pointed out. "How are you feeling?"

"You... you were the boy in the market. You gave me the soap." I took a breath, letting all the scrambled memories slide back into place. I looked down at myself and saw I was in pale green scrubs with a white cotton blanket laid over my legs. "I... I'm dizzy and tired." I finally answered. My left arm was exposed and the lines looked worse than ever. Thin quartz lines wrapped around my hand and were spreading past my elbow. I pulled the blanket over it. "Where are my clothes?"

Merlin nodded towards a cabinet in the corner of the room. "In there. One of the nurses had them cleaned for you."

I swung my legs over the side of the bed and made some hesitant steps towards the cabinet. I wasn't as weak as I was in the clinic, but I suspected Merlin was watching something akin to a young Bambi. As he said, my clothes were in the cabinet folded in a neat pile with my bracelet sitting on top. "Where's my bag?"

Merlin rubbed the back of his neck, "It wasn't in your pod room. They must have taken it when you were brought into the healing facility. We weren't really in a position for a leisurely look around the place. Was there anything important in there?"

I shook my head, "It was just food and supplies. Nothing much." It had been my lifeline in the wilds. It was one of my few belongings from my life. At least I still had the bracelet. I slipped it on my wrist and gathered up the rest of my clothes before heading back over to the bed.

"I'm sure we can replace everything. Just make a list. I'll see what I can do."

While it would be nice to have everything replaced, I wondered where he was going to get it all. Whoever those people were who rescued me from the treatment centre, they likely didn't have New Atlantis ration accounts. But if he could, it would be nice to have a store of supplies just in case I needed to run again. "Sure, it would only be a few basics." I played with my bracelet, "Where am I?"

"With friends." Merlin pulled the collar of his shirt down, just enough for me to see a patch of translucent skin with the refractive rippling texture of water. At the edge of the fabric, I could just see a little of his heart pumping within his chest.

My eyes widened, "You have it too." I felt a single beating ache in my arm, "Why... why did you stop them from giving me the cure?"

"Because you didn't want it," Merlin replied simply as if it were the most obvious thing in the world. "I saw you at the market, you were hiding from them. Most sick people would have run to them like bees to honeysuckle."

If it wasn't for Grey I would have gone to New Atlantis the moment I was sick. I wanted to. If he hadn't stopped me, I would have

36

been cured by now and back home with my parents. He would still be alive. "What can I say...I've heard things." I murmured. Not wanting to think about it, I wrangled the topic back to...wherever I was. "What about the others who were with you? Were they all sick too?"

"Yeah. In a way. Most of us here are."

"Here being...?"

Merlin made a grand gesture around the room. "We are the resistance."

So much for not thinking about Grey. I remembered Grey's blind fury and shutting off the TV after a news article about protesters came on. It was all I could do not to wince as the sound of gunshots ricocheted through my head. "You were on the news. They said you were protesting the cure."

"Yep. That's us." A grin pulled at Merlin's lips as he sat up a little straighter, like a puppy waiting for his reward. "Well, most of those cases are us. I'm not sure what you already know about that farce New Atlantis is calling a cure but there's more to it then they're saying. Marcus, he's the guy who started this rebellion, he used to work for them. He knows."

"What is the cure exactly?" I couldn't keep the tremor from my voice. Grey had told me to not get the cure though he never had time to explain. I thought back to the clinic and the room of healing pods. Grey had said they only took the disease, not cure it.

"Their 'cure'," Merlin raised his hands and made quotation marks in the air, "Is to suck the disease out of you. It's exacted in the form of Essence."

My jaw slackened. Essence was the power source for, well, everything. "You don't mean that all those people- New Atlantis are just using them like batteries?"

"Well more like oil reserves. Humans themselves are pretty horrible conductors of electricity. Man 'The Matrix' had a horrible premise." Merlin corrected. It occurred to me that Grey used to say the same thing. "At some point, New Atlantis found out that Telluria in its raw form was an extremely powerful energy source. Everyone was so happy for a cure, Everyone was so happy for a cure. Strange isn't it that Essence was 'discovered' around the same time."

It all made sense. At least in the way conspiracy theories made sense if you focused in on singular details. "But that's not... so bad," I replied tentatively. "In a way, you are just paying Essence for the cure." It did make sense. But what was this feeling still in the pit of my stomach? Grey wouldn't die only for this.

Merlin laced his fingers together and laid his hands on his lap. "That's not all." His voice was soft but strained. "It... changes you."

I bit my lip, "Changes you how?" But I already knew. Grey, my parents, after the cure they all seemed a little...off.

"Marcus would be able to explain it better..." Merlin hesitated.

"Tell me, please." I didn't know who this Marcus guy was. I would much rather hear it from Merlin. He seemed trustworthy at least.

He pushed a hand through his black hair, "When Telluria is extracted completely, something...snaps. I've seen it. What comes out of those pods are more monster than human."

"It breaks you," I repeated the words I heard what felt like an aeon ago. "How are the streets not filled with raging monsters then?"

"That's the last part of the 'cure'." Again Merlin raised his hands in mock air quotes. "Marcus says they inject something in the base of your brain, like a nanocomputer. It controls the impulses, makes you normal. It's not perfect, but it fools most people."

My body was shaking. The thin lines on my arm were starting to ache and I looked to Merlin. He was sitting slightly forward, his shoulders tight and his face drawn into a mixed expression of disgust and concern. "They use it to control people too... don't they?" I asked, barely loud enough to break the silence.

Silent, he nodded.

I thought back to Grey. He kept apologizing, saying he couldn't help calling New Atlantis while pushing me to run at the same time. I remembered him wincing in pain, struggling to warn me. "It makes people report to New Atlantis if they see a mark, doesn't it? And if they resist, it hurts them. Doesn't it?"

Again he nodded. Calm as still water, he looked up at me, "I saw a news bulletin about you. It's okay, you don't need to tell me what happened. But... it's not like they say, is it? You didn't kill that boy."

I blinked back a fresh flurry of tears, "N-no."

He offered a soft smile, "We protest and rebel because we're trying to stop them. Or at least, get New Atlantis to disclose what they're doing. There is another way to treat Telluria. People should have a choice don't you think?"

I let out a hollow laugh. Soul or body, either way, seemed like death. I didn't want to slowly turn into stone. "What is it?" I whispered, wiping away the angry tears. "If it's anything like their cure, no thanks."

"It's not a cure." Merlin corrected. "Think of it more as a kind of therapy?" He rolled back the sleeves of his buttoned shirt. "I'm going to show you something, okay? Try not to scream. It's really not good for your vocal chords."

When I nodded, Merlin rubbed his hands together. He pulled his hands apart slowly. There was something clear and rippling forming between his palms. Water, I realized with a shock. Tiny droplets were fusing together, pulling from all directions as if Merlin were gathering the moisture from the air. Together the droplets formed a small floating sphere of water.

The sphere floated closer to me, seemingly controlled by Merlin. I reached out a tentative hand and poked it.

Merlin chuckled lightly and let the waterfall free. It splashed through my hands, before returning to Merlin and forming a sphere once again. "This is our cure. And this is our gift."

I grabbed my sweater and stumbled from the bed. "Get away." This was crazy. This couldn't be real. I moved as far away from Merlin as I could manage, pushing myself into a far corner. "Get away!"

"Hey, hey it's okay. Miss... ah... I never caught your name?" Merlin put his hands out. The sphere of water evaporated in mid-air. He got up from his chair and crossed the room to me. He kept his hands up and stopped several feet away from me.

I squeezed my back against the wall, "What. Was. That." I demanded with every breath. I shouldn't have moved so quickly. My legs were threatening to give way beneath me.

"It's just water." I flinched as another small sphere formed. The sphere floated into Merlin's mouth and he swallowed it. "See? Just water."

I decided at that point that no, my legs weren't going to hold me. I slid to the floor. Merlin followed suit, sitting on the floor where he had been standing, keeping a careful distance from me.

When he looked convinced that I wasn't going to faint, he continued, "I was freaked out too at first. Most people are. The last one who came through was convinced we slipped him some LSD."

I took a moment to catch my breath. Merlin to his credit was being patient during all this. I had the feeling that this wasn't his first time explaining this to someone. "The sickness makes us do that?" I gestured vaguely in the direction of Merlin.

Merlin gave a little nod. "Try not to be afraid of it. It's really more of a blessing than a curse." To illustrate his point, he pulled more water from the air. It took the shape of a beta fish that swam around his head. "This is our cure. This is what the illness is. If I were to let Telluria just run its course, I would have been a puddle years ago. But by using the same power New Atlantis would have extracted, it stops the spread. Reverses it sometimes. That patch on my chest used to cover my entire torso."

I covered my arm with my sweater. "I...I don't know how to do...any of that." More correctly, I didn't want to.

40

"But you already have." Merlin pointed out. I must have looked surprised since he continued, "Under your pod. Didn't you see it?"

I shook my head, "I was a little busy at the time."

"There was a cluster of stone spikes under your pod in the healing facility. One looked like it had pierced it. I'm surprised you didn't notice. You at least had to feel them form, it was like a small earthquake. We felt it from the other end of the hallway. It's how we found you so fast."

I glanced up at him, "There was something sharp inside the pod. I cut the first strap on it."

"It happens sometimes. If you're scared enough. Things will just happen."

I twisted my bracelet around my wrist, "There was a cave, near my house when I first ran away. I know those woods, there was never a cave there before."

The beta fish did a little loop de loop in the air, "Exactly."

"But I can't control it! It just... happens." I began to protest, but Merlin raised his hands.

"You can't control it yet," he pointed out. "That's alright, we can teach you. Well if you want. You don't have to, but the alternative is rather grim."

I hugged my left arm to my body. It still hurt, as if it wanted me to do something like Merlin's beta fish.

Merlin stood up and reached his hand out to me. The beta fish faded back into the air. "Speaking of which, there is someone you ought to meet. Here, let me help you back into bed. Marcus will murder me if he thinks I scared you too badly."

I took his hand and stood back on unsteady legs. He helped me back to the bed where I sat down. Merlin crossed the room to the door, "I'll be right back." He opened the door but paused in the frame.

Outside was a white empty hall lit by bright fluorescent bulbs. "You know, you never did tell me your name."

"Terra Chase."

"It is a pleasure to make your acquaintance Miss Chase." Merlin made a mockery of a bow, blue eyes alight with mirth. In spite of myself, I smiled. "Merlin Spencer at your service." And then he slipped out the door, closing it gently behind him.

Once I was alone, I swung my legs over the side of the bed again. I took the time to get a better view of my surroundings. A clinical looking room, it had white walls and a blue linoleum floor that was speckled white like a robins egg. The bed was old and brass, with various bits of doctoring equipment held in a panel over my head. There was a bedside table, a simple white thing with a single empty drawer. The cabinet where my clothes had been had some upper shelves. They were lined with gloves, bandages, fluid-filled vials, and clean syringes. A yellow and orange biohazard disposal hung from the side of the cabinet.

While Merlin was gone, I put on my shoes, socks and sweater. I found a spare trash bag in the cabinet and used it to stash my other clothes. After a moment of thought, I added a roll of bandages, some rubber gloves, a vial labelled penicillin, and one syringe. I hid the medical supplies in the legs of my rolled up jeans. I felt I could trust Merlin, he did help me twice now. But the rest of these people, I wasn't sure yet. It felt better to have a plan B in any case.

By the time Merlin returned, I was sitting on the bed again with my belongings stowed under my pillow. Merlin was accompanied by a man. He was tall and broad with salt and pepper hair that I guessed must have once been very dark. His features were hard and sharp as if he were cut from stone.

"Terra, this is Marcus. Marcus is our founder and is in charge of most things. Marcus, this is Terra." Merlin gestured between us in an introduction. His role finished, he strolled over to the side wall and leaned against it.

Marcus was left with the chair. He sat down to face me. "Type E. From the St. Catherine's raid?" Marcus asked. His voice was deep and rumbled through his chest.

"Yes, Sir. New Atlantis caught me in Niagara." In lieu of knowing any actual title, Sir seemed appropriate enough. Marcus didn't seem to mind in any case.

"And Merlin says that you initially tried to run from the New Atlantis officers? Even though you clearly have been infected for, I'm going to guess about two weeks. Why is that?"

My jaw tightened. "I don't trust them." I didn't really want to get into the specifics.

"Yes but why?" Marcus had the tone of voice like he was talking to a child, "Please understand Miss Chase that we normally have to educate those we find first. It is quite strange to find someone who is already distrusting of New Atlantis. Aside from someone naturally prone to paranoia, but I feel that is not the case with you."

I looked at him, just looked at him, straight in his dark hard eyes.

"I see." He murmured softly as if I had told him everything. "Someday perhaps, you will share your story." He laced his hands together in front of him, relenting. "But for now, I trust Merlin has already told you a little about us?"

"More like showed." I corrected, making Merlin snort.

Marcus raised an eyebrow at Merlin but made no further comment. "And what did you think?"

"It's impossible." That was the first of a long list of adjectives I had in mind. "But the evidence suggests otherwise."

"A wise woman." Marcus seemed almost relieved by how very sensible I was being. What could I say? I was raised by a scientist. "And do you understand what this means for yourself?"

The mark on my arm was pulsing but I resisted the urge to pull it closer. "I'm Type E. Meaning my own... abilities... will be earth based. Rocks and stuff."

"And that you must use them." Marcus placed his hands on his knees. "It is the only way to keep Telluria from consuming you aside from the use of a pod."

In spite of myself, I shuddered. "What is it? Magic?" It was ludicrous. All of it.

Marcus shook his head. "I do not believe so. More like a borrowed energy. Though it is uncertain how it came to be inside human bodies."

"Merlin said it's Essence." As tired as I was at the time, I remember seeing the essence in the healing facility and in my own pod. Though at the time I assumed it was being pumped in, not extracted out.

"Essence as you know it is nothing more or less, then the purest energy of the earth. New Atlantis believes that it is the very life force of this planet. Something so primordial and ancient, has Merlin told you what happens when it is ripped from your body?"

I nodded, though I preferred not to be having this conversation a second time. I could see the ghosts just behind Marcus's eyes, and I was almost certain he would see Grey in mine.

"It breaks you, Miss Chase. You fail to be human. Imagine someone you love. Imagine them without empathy, without feeling. They walk and talk and act, but what made them human is gone. Or at least, that's how they would be without New Atlantis interference. Now the cured are little more than their devoted sheep."

I was cold, chilled to the marrow which had nothing to do with the temperature in the room. "Merlin told me all this. About the cure. About the implant. Everything."

Marcus made an approving noise in the back of his throat. "Well then, did you have any questions, Miss Chase?"

44

"Would someone be able to fight the compulsion? If they didn't want to do what New Atlantis programmed them to do. Say, to warn others?"

Marcus sighed heavily and shook his head. "Sadly, no. Once the Essence is gone, it's gone. Even if someone could fight it, there's no caring left in them to bother warning someone."

Don't get the cure! Run! I had to call them! Run! I shut my eyes against the screaming in my head.

"We can talk more on this later. For now, however, there are other things to discuss. Your training." Marcus didn't seem to notice my distress, or simply didn't care. "We have people who can teach you how to control your abilities, but there is a price."

I took a breath and opened my eyes, "What is it?" My voice sounded hollow in my ears. I didn't have much to trade, aside from the clothes on my back.

"We are a force, Terra Chase. And as such, we need manpower." Marcus crossed his arms, "Six months of service for our cause. Help us spread the word of what New Atlantis is doing. Help us resist the cure."

I raised my chin, staring him down from where I sat. "And if hypothetically I refused?"

Marcus shrugged and gestured to the room. "Then we will make your last days pass in comfort."

#

Marcus and Merlin both left to give me time to decide. But not without locking the door from the outside. I suspected it was to keep me from escaping and running to New Atlantis. Two days past as I took my time deciding what to do. That didn't stop me from building my supplies. Nurses came with food sometimes, I always hid a little of it away, along with the medical supplies I already stole.

Sometimes Merlin came to visit. He never mentioned the choice to be made so we talked about simple things. What time of day it was,

45

what the weather was like, or any interesting outside news. Apparently, London was reopening the Globe Theatre. New Atlantis was starting to reintroduce true currency into the marketplace. We talked about things far away and impersonal. If there was any news about my family or my home, he didn't mention it and I didn't ask.

When I was alone, there was nothing stopping me from lingering on the past few weeks of my life. I found myself watching the marks on my arm. I could almost see them move, undulating and crawling across my skin like so many spider legs. How long would it take? What would it feel like? I knew it didn't hurt. Even my Mother never felt pain when there was a fire burning just beneath her skin.

Grey's marks had never made it that far. His had only just crawled over his shoulder when New Atlantis took him away. He was smiling that day. He hugged his mom goodbye and then me. His eyes were bright and hopeful. Everything would be okay. Why wouldn't it be?

It was that light that was missing when he came home. Grey had left, and what came home was a dull shadow of him. I curled up under my thin blanket, trying to remember the days before he got sick. My mind kept flickering back to those last moments. To the Grey of my childhood, to the Grey forced to kneel in his kitchen.

A bang ran through the room. I bolted up with a scream caught in my throat.

"Hey, it's okay. It's just me." Merlin came into the room balancing a tray in his hands. He set it down on my bedside table. There was chicken soup thick with rice and vegetables, a slice of crusty bread, and a fresh pitcher of water with a glass.

"I... I thought..." Opting not to finish that sentence, I reached for the water and poured myself a glass. The glass felt cool and smooth between my palms. I took a sip, waiting for my heart to come back down to a steady trot. "It was nothing. Just a nightmare." I told him eventually one I felt controlled enough. It wasn't his fault every loud noise sounded like a gun.

"Wanna talk about it?" He pulled up the folding metal chair, straddled it and crossed his arms over the back. "People say I'm a good listener. Though then again, it's also sort of my job." He flashed a bright easy smile that I was starting to think was a staple of his.

I traded the water for bread. I held it in both hands, tearing off small chunks of crust to nibble on. I did this methodically, going all around the edge until the crust was gone and just soft bread remained. "Marcus wasn't right. The cured can sometimes fight the compulsion."

His smile wavered. "But that's impossible-"

"No, it's not. I saw it." I looked up at him, "My friend Grey. We grew up together, we were friends for as long as I can remember. He was cured a couple weeks ago. When he came home, he was... different. Like Marcus said, he was Grey but he wasn't." I looked back at my bread. I tore off a tiny piece, rolling it like clay between my fingers. "We were having a sleepover. In hindsight, I'm not sure how I didn't notice I was sick. I just felt so tired. The mark formed in the middle of the night I guess. Grey saw it and woke me." I put the bread down. This part seemed important somehow. "He told me to run. He was the one who told me not to get the cure. They take it, they don't cure it. He said that over and over again."

Merlin's brow was chased. I could see him trying to make sense of what I said.

"He told me that he couldn't help it, that he had to call them. They were coming and I had to run. I didn't understand any of it and he was just pushing me out the door. And th-then they came and-" My hands were shaking so much I fisted them in the blankets. I didn't know if Merlin noticed or not. "They came and they..." I took a breath. "They shot him."

It just tumbled out, after that, I couldn't seem to stop. I told Merlin everything; hiding in the woods, the cave that just appeared, travelling south, reaching Niagara and getting captured. I told my story rigid as a bone. My hands fisted in the blankets, anchoring me in place. For his part, Merlin was a good listener. He didn't interrupt and he made all the appropriate nods and noises in all the right places. Best of all I think, I was able to just say my piece. He didn't ask questions, he didn't say that I didn't need to keep going if I was upset. He just let me say as much or as little as I needed.

At the end, I pulled my knees up to my chest and rested my chin atop them. "Please don't tell Marcus any of it. I... I'm not sure I trust him."

Merlin gave a little shrug, "Not my story to tell." He said easily. "Though... you might want to consider telling him yourself some time." He put a hand up at the incredulous expression on my face, "Not all of it mind. But he would be very interested in Grey. I've never heard of someone fighting the compulsion before. And the fact they silenced him to make it look like you killed him. It's one of those things that could really help the movement you know if more people knew."

A knot was working between my shoulder blades. I didn't want the world to think that I had killed Grey in some Telluria enraged state. But at the same time, I wasn't sure how much more I really wanted to talk about it. Preferring not to dwell on it, for now, I gestured widely in the general direction of the door. "So what's it like being a part of...this."

"Like a laid back military. Sort of." Merlin shrugged, "We're a team. We do what we can to help the sick, we recruit who we can, we spread the word, and we occasionally sabotage healing centres." As he grinned there was a wild gleam in his eyes, "And from time to time we rescue people like you from being cured. Which... may or may not have included hijacking one of their vans."

I raised an eyebrow. I remembered the van, not much after though. "What about the training. Is it difficult?" I held my arms a little tighter, "Still seems like magic to me."

"Naw it's easy to get the idea. Especially if you've already done it before. Accidentally or no." Merlin conjured another one of his water creations, this time a robin flying around the room. Droplets of water flecked off its tiny wings with each beat and flew back around to rejoin with the rest of the bird. "It's like any muscle. Once you realize it's there, it's just a matter of exercising it."

48

"But I didn't control it. Those things I did just... happened. I don't know how. I'm not sure I even believe it was me at all." If it wasn't for the cave and the pillars in the healing centre, I wasn't sure I could believe any of it.

"Eh well. Minor detail. Learning how to tap into it is where everyone starts. You have to focus through your mark see-" then he stopped and shook his head. "Mind you, you're not going to want to try it here. We have training rooms built special for any kind of shenanigans your powers might get up to in your fledgeling use."

That gave me some pause. "Such as?"

"Well..." His grin turned sheepish, "I'm not going to name names, but a certain leader of ours broke some windows by tossing rocks around."

"Marcus? Really?" I giggled, "The same Marcus that was in here. Funny, I thought he could do no wrong. He certainly seems to think he's on a first name basis with the President of New Atlantis."

"Hey come now. He's not so bad really." The look I gave Merlin was so incredulous he put his hands up in defence, "I know he's a little, shall we say prickly, when you first meet him. But it's only because he is so passionate about spreading the truth about New Atlantis. That and keeping us safe from them. Think of him as a hedgehog."

I slid my legs back down and leaned against the pillows. I crossed my arms over my chest, "I want to talk to the hedgehog."

Merlin perked up a little, "Does this mean you plan on joining?"

I looked up at him, "On my terms."

#

For the leader of a large and highly organized rebellion organization, it didn't take Marcus long to arrive. In the hour while I waited, I got out of bed, dressed in my clean clothes, finger brushed my hair, and made the bed. When he arrived I was sitting on the edge of the bed with my sweater folded neatly on my lap and my pilfered supplies tucked within it. Just in case.

49

"Merlin said you wanted to speak with me. You have come to a decision then." It was not a question.

I nodded, "I have," I raised my chin just a little, "Though I have some conditions of my own."

"The length of minimum service is not up for negotiation if that is what you are implying."

"No, it's not that." I gestured to the chair for him to sit. "There are some things I want if I join you. And in return, I have something that you want."

Marcus sat at ease, his hands held loosely in his lap. "Alright, Miss Chase. You tell me your terms."

I took a breath. "I will agree to join for the minimum six months. But after that, do I have your word that I will be free to leave? If I choose."

"You do. Though... I should say that that is already part of the deal." Marcus pointed out. "After six months you may stay as long as you like, or leave if that is your choice.

"I know. I just wanted your word. It feels less like my hand is being forced if there's an exit strategy you know." I waved my hand dismissively, "Here is what I want besides that. First, I want to know of my family. We both know that I can't go home, maybe never. So I just want someone to make sure that my parents are okay and Mrs McNair. She's my neighbour and she's never been sick. I just want to make sure New Atlantis hasn't done anything to her. You have my blessing to talk her over to the dark side if you want. Even if the idea of Mrs McNair as a rebel fighter was laughable. At least she would have a way out if New Atlantis was mistreating her.

"Also, I want to know what New Atlantis is saying about me." I slid my hands under my legs. I squeezed my hands together, feeling my nails dig into my palms. I kept my head held high, despite everything in me wanting to shut up now. "In return, I will tell you about my friend Grey. H-he was sick and cured. He fought the compulsion."

Marcus leaned forward slightly. I had him. I knew it. I could see how much he wanted that information by the shine in his eyes. "What you ask will not be easy Miss Chase. New Atlantis is likely watching your home closely." He paused though, considering the offer, "But... I have heard the rumours of what happened to your friend. I am very curious to know the true events as they occurred. Very well then. I will accept your terms, Miss Chase. Does this mean that you are joining us officially?"

I nodded. "For Grey."

Marcus stood and offered his hand. I did likewise and we shook in agreement, "May I be the first to welcome you to the team, Miss Chase."

CHAPTER FIVE

A New Beginning

I told Marcus everything about Grey. I had hoped that the second retelling would be easier, seeing as I just told it all to Merlin. It wasn't. My voice choked when I mentioned the shot. My body tensed as if the gun were right there, pointing at my head. Marcus seemed pleased. In the same way that a biologist is pleased when they have a new specimen to play with. I gave Marcus a puzzle to poke at and pick apart until it revealed itself to him. Hopefully, it would be of some use. This was all for Grey after all. I couldn't let his sacrifice go in vain. He didn't scream at me to run so that I could die a slow stony death in a hospital bed.

I technically had to stay in that room for another day. "Just standard procedure Miss Chase. The healing staff will want a check-up before you are released. And it gives me time to make the final arrangements for your stay," Marcus told me before leaving.

Merlin was ecstatic. "You're going to love it! Or well I hope you do. The people here are pretty great. And it beats hiding in the woods doesn't it?"

The more I thought about it, the more I realized Merlin was really made for his job. His enthusiasm for the rebellion was infectious. He was convinced that I would want to stay at least a little longer after the initial six months. I wasn't so sure about that, but I kept my doubts to myself.

Merlin came to fetch me bright and early the next morning. I was barely finished breakfast when he came swooping in. "Ready to go?

I thought we could go see your room first. Your roommate is a friend of mine and she's dying to meet you. She took the morning off and everything."

"I have a roommate?" Was the only reply I could think of to the long list of questions forming in my mind.

"Oh yeah. Marcus believes in the buddy system," Merlin said as if that explained everything.

"Right. Let's go meet her then." I pulled on my sweater which still had the small supply of food in the front pocket. Most of the medical supplies I put back in the cupboard the day before. It was too hard to hide them without a bag. I drew a line at wasting food, however.

Walking to the door, Merlin opened it and stepped aside. "After you m'lady."

"Terra is fine you know." After I passed through the doorway, he fell into step beside me and led me down some long brightly lit hallways. Everything was white walls and generic tiled floors. There was a general lack of windows, and lines of pipes ran along the walls. "Are we underground?"

"An old military bunker. It belonged to this old rich guy who thought the world was going to break into World War 3. Well, he wasn't far off I guess. But still, I think he went a little overboard. This place is massive."

"What happened to him?"

Merlin hesitated a moment. "Died. Faded into a gust of wind."

A silence fell between us. It was strange to think that could happen to either of us if Marcus's treatment stopped working at any said moment. "So what's my roommate like? You said you were friends?"

The easy smile returned to Merlin's face. "Sure she's great. Her name is Ember. Sweetest girl you'll ever meet with the temper of a hurricane." He directed us down a hallway of doors. Each door was decorated with a small brass plate containing a room number and the names of the occupants inside.

"Ah..."

"Don't worry. It's almost always directed at her brother." We came to the second last door in the hallway. "Here we are. Your room."

Despite the fact that my name was indeed on the door, 'T. Chase', Merlin knocked. The girl who answered was, in a word, gorgeous. She was tall and lean with red hair cascading down her back in loose curls. Her face was angular, with a small scar on her left temple. The most striking thing about her eyes. They were the colour of amber left out in the sunlight. Fire danced behind them in a way that had nothing to do with the lighting in the room.

"Ember, this is Terra. Terra, Ember," Merlin waved his hand between us in way of introduction.

Ember thrust her hand forward and shook mine. I was a little surprised by how rough and calloused it was. "Hello," she said with a beaming smile and pulled me inside. The room, like the hall, was painted white, but it felt more lived in. Half the walls were covered in drawings and cuttings from books. There were two old brass beds, one against either wall. One bed was sporting a floral duvet and the other had a small pile of clothes on it. At the foot of each bed was a trunk.

"That bed is yours," Ember pointed at the one with the clothes, "father said you didn't have much with you, so those are some things of mine that you can have if they fit. The trunk is for your stuff, and there's extra bedding in there." She pivoted and pointed at the second door in the room "And that there is our bathroom."

"Um... thanks," I wasn't sure what else to say really. Everything was getting really real, really fast. "You said your father told you?" I wondered which one of the healers he was. It was nice of him, whoever it was.

"Mhmm," her curls bounced as she nodded, "Marcus."

The laugh that started in my throat came out like a weird strangled cough. "M-Marcus is your father?" Oh, joy. I could only imagine he arranged this to keep an eye on me.

The fire in Ember's eyes glowed warm with mirth, "You know he's not so bad when you get to know him," she said as if she were used to this sort of reaction. "He's like a- Merlin what's that simile you use?"

"Hedgehog," Merlin answered from the door. He was leaning against the frame.

"Yes, indeed a hedgehog. Though I was rather fond of pineapple as well," she sighed and turned on Merlin. "Well, have you given her the grand tour yet?"

"Nope. Was just starting. Wanna come along?" Merlin pushed himself off the door frame and shoved his hands in his pockets.

"Most certainly." Ember looped her arm through mine and steered me out of the room, "I have seniority over both of you after all. In all reality, I should be the one giving the tour."

Merlin fell into step behind us. "So long as you don't mind me tagging along. You don't do you, Terra?"

It was a little unsettling how straightforward she was, but it was a nice change not having to constantly think about my next move. "I... ah... sure?" I didn't mean for my voice to inflect.

"Perfect." Ember tugged me along down the hall. "We'll do all the boring stuff first."

#

The base, as I came to find out, was huge. Merlin was not exaggerating in the slightest. It was an old military bunker that the original owner was in the process of renovating before he died. The main base was all deep underground and was designed to be safe from most possible disasters. But since the rich liked to like in luxury more often than not, he also built a mansion on the surface.

56

Ember brought us down more long halls of doors. "These are the other dorms. The tunnels go on for ages. Not all of it has been renovated yet but we're working on it. We can house a couple hundred at the moment," Her voice swelled with pride.

"Is that what you do?" She definitely had the hands of a woman familiar with manual labour.

"Me? Oh no. I mean from time to time if things are slow perhaps, but I have my own things to do," Ember explained without elaborating.

Merlin walked behind us, hands in his pockets, whistling tunelessly. We went down another hall. I realized that this was the way Merlin and I came before. Ember pointed towards the brass plates on the doors. "This hall is mostly offices. Sickbay is at the end. But I'm sure you saw enough of that for now. Come on."

Next was the dining hall, a large open room with tables and benches. A glass and metal counter along the far wall separated the eating area from the kitchen. It wasn't meal time yet but I could smell garlic and basil wafting from the kitchen.

From there we went up a couple flights of steps. "We're nearly at the surface. Just under it really." Ember told us. We went into a spacious vehicle hanger. They had a little of everything: from motorcycles, to utility trucks, to a small private jet tucked away in the back corner. I wondered where they possibly found the gasoline for them all, or if they were Essence engines. Knowing what I know now, Essence seemed unlikely. Maybe electric? Towards the back of the hanger was the workshop. The air trilled with someone using a pneumatic drill nearby. Ember patted the hydraulic lift almost tenderly. "This is what I do. A couple others and I keep everything in working order."

My jaw slackened. Of all things that I guessed Ember might do, this was not it.

"Now don't give me that look." Ember chastised playfully. "Didn't your Mama ever tell you not to judge a book by its cover?"

I had the sense to look bashful. "Sorry."

Ember flipped her hair and shrugged. "Father used to work on machines. He's an office man now, but he used to bring me to work with him and let me pass him his tools. It just grew from there."

"Okay, I get that." If anything, I could understand learning from a parent. My dad was a botanist. I doubted I would have survived long if I hadn't known just about every edible plant in the region of home.

Ember looped her arm through mine again and directed us out of the hanger and back into the base proper. She gestured to another set of stairs that led up. "That way is the surface. We don't really use the mansion above. Father says New Atlantis would find us faster is the whole place was lit up."

"Seems like a waste," I said looking in the general direction of the stairs.

"It's not completely unused. The generator is stored up there. There's a pretty nice library too."

"Well, and the last Christmas party," Merlin amended, a roguish grin pulling on his lips that made me wonder what kind of Christmas party it was.

"Oh, that was lovely," Ember's voice was soft and floating like a dream.

Ember led onwards to the last leg of the tour. I found myself at the crossroads of four rooms. Each had long windows that gave a full view of what was going on inside. There was a room for each of the four Tellurian types. The Earth room was filled with stones and sand. A woman stood in the room sculpting stone like it was play dough. The Fire room had burning braziers and scorched walls. The boy inside was concentrating on a ball of flame in his hands. Water had a fountain and a skim of water on the floor. A middle-aged man was swimming laps in a pool that moved around the room with him. Ember stopped at the last room and waved at the occupant inside. Air had giant fans built into the walls. The young man Ember was waving to was sitting in a meditative position. His eyes were closed and his legs were folded beneath him. He hovered several feet off the ground while the wind in the room whipped at his clothes and golden hair.

"The training rooms," Merlin explained. He was standing next to me, also watching the levitating boy with the light of amusement in his eyes. "One for each type. Marcus thinks that it helps you to learn if you're isolated with your element."

"And does it?"

"Well," he tilted his head, "in the beginning sure. But once you get the hang of it, it stops to really matter. Until you master it, it's still encouraged to use the training rooms though. It's safer. They're made to withstand whatever we can possibly throw at them. Within reason anyway."

Ember came skipping back towards us. "Cy is just coming down now," She gestured towards the levitating boy.

The boy was stretching out of his seated position, lengthening his long legs until his feet touched the floor. The moment he was on solid ground, the wind died within the chamber, and his gold coloured hair fell in a windswept heap on his head. He stepped out of the room and came towards us. Like Ember, he was tall, at least a head over me, with hazel eyes.

"Terra this is my older brother Cyrus," Ember said once Cyrus had joined our little group.

"So you're the one they got from the St. Catherine's raid. Father was telling me about it earlier." Cyrus offered his hand to shake. He had a firm hold and shook hands the same way as his father. "Pleased to meet you."

"Likewise." I shook out my hand a little once I had it back. "That was, um, impressive. What you were doing in there."

"Oh," he rubbed the back of his neck, "just something I've been working on."

"Cyrus wants to fly," Ember elaborated. "You should be able to do it by now, though. How long were you hovering there before we came along?"

Cyrus rolled his shoulders. "Mmm... about an hour. But sitting in place and flying are two very different things Em."

Ember waved her hand dismissively, "sure sure whatever you say."

I watched the people in the other three rooms. The little boy was bouncing his fireball against the wall, adding to the collection of scorch marks. "What's next?" I finally asked. Despite the short tour, there was a weariness in my voice. It was dizzying to see the sorts of things these people, people like me I amended, could do.

"Mmm... well, that's it really. Tour wise." Ember turned to me, "Any questions?"

I was still looking at the four rooms. "Marcus said I would be here for six months minimum. What will I even be doing? He didn't say."

"Mmm come on. Let's go back to the room and talk about it. Would you like to come too, Cy?"

"No, you go on. I wanted to stay here a little longer." Cyrus motioned back to the air room.

Ember shrugged and linked arms with me, "Suit yourself Cy. See you at dinner."

The three of us went back to mine and Ember's room. There, Merlin and Ember told me everything that I could possibly think of asking. New recruits were cycled through the organization. Everyone had to learn the basics of everything until the third month when they received their permanent assignment. Merlin said that tomorrow he would get my schedule for me though every day followed a similar format. In the mornings I would be training in the element rooms. In the afternoon I would be in a different place every day. One day I might be in the med bay, the next with Ember in the vehicle workshop. There was also helping in renovations, cleaning, cooking, office work, or the gardens. I already knew I would be good in the gardens. It wouldn't be such a bad existence here if I could just do that. Some of the other jobs though, I had never even touched a car before.

"Don't worry about it. You'll be taught everything you need to know," Merlin soothed after I expressed my doubts about being useful. "Gives everyone a fair chance you know. To see where you really shine."

"And if I don't stay? Won't it just be a waste of everyone's time?" I bit my lip. I liked Ember and Merlin so far. I didn't want them, or anyone else I befriended to feel betrayed if I left.

"Not really." Ember curled a lock of hair around her finger. "You would have been a help for six months, and you'll leave better equipped to survive out there then you did when you came in. It's your choice, Terra."

I got the sense that they would like it if I stayed. But I also felt that they tried not to hang their hopes on the idea. How many people I wondered actually stayed after six months. How many left forever?

#

The next morning, Ember brought me down to the dining hall for breakfast. It was crowded, the room filled with the cacophony of noise that came with at least a hundred people sitting, talking and eating. As we made our way to the line of people waiting for food, I tried to ignore the one thing that had been nagging me since the day before. Everyone had a mark. It should have been obvious, but for some reason, the stark unhidden truth of it was jarring. There was a man with a bald head so transparent that I could see the soft twisting curl of his brain beneath his skull. There was a girl with limestone scales layered down the left side of her face. I kept my head down pressing my bare arm against my leg wishing that I had worn a sweater. I was wearing a t-shirt and yoga pants, Ember's recommended outfit for my first day of training. Both she and Merlin had warned me that using my power would be strenuous at first.

Ember, noticing my reaction, leaned to whisper in my ear. "You get used to it. No one will be afraid of seeing your mark here." Her eyes, like amber in a fire, glittered.

61

I twisted my fingers around the end of my braided hair. "Doesn't it ever go away?" I had hoped somehow that it would.

"No," Ember sounded apologetic. "It gets smaller, it fades. But it'll never be gone forever," She sighed and glanced at her reflection in the glass of the serving counter. "A reminder I suppose."

By then it was our turn to get our breakfast. There were oats and fruit, and much to my surprise, coffee. "How..."

"Don't expect it every day. There are small rebellions all over the world. Sometimes we trade with them." Ember explained.

Once we had our breakfast, instead of stopping to look for a spot, Ember walked towards the back left corner of the room. It was her usual table, Merlin and Cyrus were already there. Cyrus was digging into his own oats. A freshly showered Merlin was beside him, hands moving as he talked.

I sat down across from them, Ember beside me. "What are you talking about?" I asked.

"Oh! I got a new assignment today. I'm going to Florida after breakfast," Merlin's eyes were alight with excitement. "Josh told me - he's the recruitment leader - that there's a whole group there protesting the cure. They say friends and family who got it were never the same after. There's even a rumour that one of the cured warned them. Like your fri-" Merlin stopped when he saw my panic-stricken face. "Sorry. Just, this is good news. The more people resisting, the more people will eventually know the truth. Marcus has been talking about setting up another base for so long and the Florida group has got to be enough."

I stirred my oatmeal. There were blueberries in it and flecks of fruit were turning the whole thing blue. "It's pretty rare isn't it, to have the cured say anything? Marcus seemed to think it was impossible."

It wasn't Merlin who replied, but Cyrus. "The compulsion is strong. Normally the cured literally can't help doing whatever New Atlantis programmed them to do. But, perhaps if a person with a strong enough will could resist a little?" Cyrus looked up at me, and I got the sneaking suspicion that his father told him more than just my name.

I looked down at my food, no longer feeling hungry. At least over the noise of the dining hall, I couldn't hear the gun.

"I've got some news too," Cyrus continued. He was finished his oats and spoke between sips of coffee. "I've been assigned as your trainer Terra."

"Me? But your Type A." I assumed that my trainer would be Type E, Earth, like me.

"I am type A. Which is why I'll be training you. We pair new recruits with their elemental opposites. Think of it as a safety net. If things get out of control, my powers will cancel out yours. The general theory is the same no matter what type you are."

My stomach shifted. He talked about things getting out of hand like it was certain to happen. "What will we be doing?"

Cyrus rolled his shoulders. "Just talking the basics today. We'll likely try a little practical work as well. Just some easy stuff," He looked up at me, "and don't look so nervous. I've trained plenty of folks. No one has spontaneously combusted or has been dragged off by witch hunters yet."

Beside me, Merlin nearly spat out his coffee. "Do you remember that one woman, ah, Clara? The one who thought for sure that we were all going to hell for our evil sorcery?"

Cyrus only half grinned and rubbed his shoulder. "I was hoping to forget about that funnily enough."

Ember leaned over to me, speaking low in my ear, "She went a little crazy and tried to stab Cy with a steak knife. He has quite the scar from it."

"What happened to her? Is she still here?" I looked around the room as if a crazy knife-wielding woman was about to run up any second now.

63

All three faces fell. "She went to Father and asked for release," Cyrus muttered. "She didn't want to be in the rebellion anymore. She wanted to wait it out."

"You don't mean-" My eyes widened as Cyrus nodded.

"I wasn't with her, she didn't want to see me. But the nurses said... they made it as comfortable as they could for her. She turned to stone at the end. She seemed more at peace with it but," he sighed heavily, "It was such a waste."

"She's the only one Cy ever lost. The other trainers lost a couple too. This..." Ember gestured at the general expanse of people in the hall, "it's too much for some people. They just can't wrap their heads around it and, well, they take the easier way."

There was a cold tingle down my spine. After watching Grey's father pass, I couldn't imagine ever choosing to wait it out.

"Ladies and Gentleman."

The room fell silent and all eyes moved in the direction of the low rumbling voice. Marcus was standing on a bench to be seen above the crowd. "I've just received word that the Florida resistance has rallied more people to the cause. The Fort Lauderdale healing centre has been stormed and shut down. Those who were in various stages of healing are being tended to. I've been in contact with their leader and it's official! We will be opening a new chapter there."

The hall erupted with applause and cheers. I sunk down in my seat, simply watching. Ember, Cyrus, and Merlin all looked ecstatic at the news, Merlin most of all. He got up and stood on the bench, whistling along with the crowd.

Marcus allowed this for a moment before raising his hands and coaxing the crowd back into silence. "Our recruitment team is going to be departing shortly. Originally, they were going to perform a simple extraction, but plans have changed. They will be taking a management team with them and helping the Florida rebellion begin their journey."

Another applause. Merlin was grinning like a Cheshire cat when he slid back down into his seat and started shovelling the rest of his breakfast into his mouth.

"Slow down. You'll give yourself indigestion," I warned him.

As if on cue, he started coughing violently and went grasping blindly for his glass of water. Crisis averted, he grinned at me. "Don't worry about me. I got a steel oesophagus." He did, however, start eating slower. "This is going to be awesome."

"How long do you think you'll be gone this time?" Cyrus was outwardly calm though I sensed he carried the same charged energy that was running throughout the room.

Merlin grinned. "When we were briefed yesterday it was a couple days. But now, probably closer to a week. Maybe two. Though I suspect the management team coming with us will be doing most of the heavy lifting."

I had a couple thoughtful spoons full of oatmeal. "What about those who were being cured?"

"They'll probably have to let anyone who had the compulsion injection go. Drive them out in the middle of nowhere and let them out. So long as they can't lead New Atlantis back to the base, they're better off," Cyrus explained. "As for the rest, Father says that so long even a small amount of Telluria remains, the person can bounce back." His brows knitted. "I don't know about those who were fully extracted, though. Father might have some Ideas. There's no coming back once it's gone completely."

"How would he know?" I tilted my head. Marcus certainly seemed to know more than the average person might.

Cyrus shrugged. "Father used to work for New Atlantis. It's not a big secret or anything. He was part of the team that developed the cure."

I sputtered, "He worked for them?!"

"Did. Past tense. But when he saw what the cure did, and the harm the compulsion caused, he left."

My mouth went dry. Just how deep was Marcus in New Atlantis before he got out?

Cyrus set his cup down and swung his legs over the side of the bench. "I've got a couple things to do before training. Terra, see you in a half hour. Merlin, good luck. See you when you get back."

"You too buddy!" Merlin waved cheerfully, then clapped me on the shoulder. "You'll be alright. Show me what Cyrus taught you when I get back eh?"

The two boys got up and left. Shortly after, so did Ember. I remained at the table a moment longer, not for the first time wondering how deep a hole I was digging myself into. And if I've already crossed the point of no return.

CHAPTER SIX

Trial and Error

Cyrus was already in the earth room when I arrived. He was making the sand swirl around like a dessert storm. He stopped when I closed the door, the sand settling back down on the floor.

"Ah, your here. Pull up a rock and sit," Cyrus gestured to one of the larger boulders in the room. I did as asked, sitting cross legged atop the offered rock. Cyrus sat across from me on his own. "So... how much as Merlin and Father already told you?"

"Just that Telluria gives you abilities that relate to the elemental type of your disease. If I use the abilities, it'll act as a cure. Ember said this morning that the mark never completely goes away. If I use these...abilities...it'll get smaller." I folded my hands together, "that's it."

Cyrus made a small noise in the back of his throat and nodded, "Alright." He stood up, grabbed a small pebble from the ground, and handed it to me. "Your element Is earth. If you were to let the illness progress, you would become earth: stone, soil, sand. Telluria has made these things as much a part of you as your lungs, your heart, your skin. That stone, to you, is like your own flesh. Just as the air is mine. That is where this all starts."

I looked down at the stone in my hand. It looked like just a stone. Smooth and flat like a river rock. I probably could have skipped it across the floor of the water room. "I'm... confused. So the rock is me and how does that help exactly?"

Cyrus gave me a rueful smile. "When you were a baby could you walk?"

"No. Neither could you I would be willing to bet."

"Exactly. You had to learn to use your legs, how to balance. When you learned to talk, you had to learn how to move all the parts of your mouth together to make the right noises. This is just the same, you're just learning to use a different muscle."

I looked from the rock to Cyrus, and back. "Okay, I get that much," trying not to sound as dubious as I felt.

Cyrus grinned. "Good. Now like most muscles, you're not going to be very strong at first. We're going to start with little things. Just moving them. You're going to start with that rock in your hand," Cyrus tilted his head. "Where's your mark?"

I turned over my left arm, exposing my wrist to show him the thin tracery of lines.

"Okay, hold the stone in that hand. It helps to focus on a spot close to your mark," He waited until I switched hands, "now start focusing on the stone. At first, you're going to need to do a lot of visualization. You need to imagine the stone as part of your hand; sixth finger, tiny arm, whatever works best for you. Focus long and hard on that. When you are ready, imagine it moving, like you would move your finger. Just try to flip it over."

I nodded, my brows knitting as I looked down at the stone. I became aware rather quickly of an uncomfortable throbbing in my wrist. It was like a second heartbeat, slower and stronger than my own. I focused on the stone through this new sensation, imagining it as an extension of my hand. It reminded me of those old movies Grey and I would watch about some young knight's apprentice being trained with a sword.

The stone moved. Though instead of flipping over, the surface rippled like water. The smooth surface turned jagged, sharpening to a point. I cried out and dropped the arrowhead from my palm.

"Huh, well that's a first," Cyrus didn't look too bothered about me not doing what he had asked. He just seemed happy that I accomplished something on my first try. Sliding from his boulder, he picked up the arrow head and brushed his thumb against the edge. It was sharp. "What were you thinking about?"

I edged away, my arm throbbing as I inched towards the door. "Kn-knight movies," I breathed and winced. The throbbing was getting stronger. "It hurts..."

Cyrus put his hands out. "Terra, deep breathes. You have to keep calm. It's a good start. Breathe..."

I shook my head violently. "H-hurts..." A hammer was slamming into my wrist.

"Terra..." Cyrus put one hand out towards me. "Terra just take a breath. Look at me. Terra look at me."

I clutched my arm as a searing pain raced up through my mark. The rock I was sitting on just moments before lurched out of the ground and threw itself across the room. Cyrus spun on his heel, putting his hands out like he meant to catch the boulder. The winds shifted and caught the boulder in mid air. Cyrus let the winds settle the rock back on the ground. Without another word, Cyrus grabbed me and hauled me out of the room.

I hugged my arm against me. My breath came in shuddering gasps. Cyrus led me over near the air room where I promptly put my back against the wall and slid to the floor. "Terra. Look at me. It's okay. You can't do anything here. It's okay."

"Wh-what did I... God, I could have killed you."

"But you didn't," Cyrus spoke gently, "you got spooked is all. Almost everyone loses control the first couple times. It's okay Terra. It's why you were paired with someone of an opposite element. I can keep things under control when that happens." The corner of his lips twitched up in the ghost of a sardonic smile. "Mind you... I think you beat a record with that boulder. But really Terra, it's okay. I had it under control."

I looked up at him. I for one didn't believe a word of it. "Does it always hurt like that?"

Cyrus shook his head. "No. It only hurt because your body tried to do too much too soon. When you turned that stone into an arrow head, did that hurt?"

I thought about it and shook my head. "That was more of a dull ache."

Cyrus nodded, "As you get stronger, you'll be able to do more without it hurting. Hell, in a few weeks you'll be able to throw all the boulders you want at me without so much as blinking an eye."

My breath caught. "No," my voice choked. "No. I don't want to throw anything. I don't want to do that again."

Cyrus lowered himself to the floor next to me and gestured to my arm. "Let me see your mark."

I turned over my wrist, exposing the tangled mess that was my mark. Only, it wasn't. It had gotten smaller. The tendrils that had started to wrap around the base of my thumb had moved back to my wrist. I pulled up the sleeve of my t-shirt. There had been a small piece winding around my shoulder that morning. It had descended back down to my elbow. The thickest of the lines, those that were around the origin, were thinner and lighter. I brushed my fingers over them. "It shrunk," I stated, dumbfounded.

"Mhmm and that is why you need to keep training. Don't give me that face. I'm guessing Father gave you the usual ultimatum. You train and use your powers, or the sickness will overcome you. Your choice. I tend to recommend training. I don't like losing people needlessly."

"I really have to come back tomorrow then?" I shivered as ice spread down my spine.

"Afraid so. It gets easier. You'll see." He clapped a hand on my shoulder "Come on. I'll walk you back to your room." Standing, Cyrus offered me his hand to help me up. I hoped he was right because I really didn't want to do that again.

70

Only things didn't get better. If anything, I got worse. Every day I would walk in that damned room and my arm would start to hurt. The moment I tried to do the smallest thing, all hell would break loose. Cyrus tried to get me to move a stone, to change its shape, to break it open, anything. He even tried taking me to the surface outside. Nothing was working.

"I'm not going to say you're hopeless." He stated as we were leaving the training room after another unsuccessful day. "You are able to do things. You just have no control yet. The important thing is you're keeping you mark small. That's all that really matters."

He was fond of giving me these sort of pep talks after we were done for the day. As if it would help me feel better. "I know," I admitted, though begrudgingly. The mark had shrunken all the way down to a band around my wrist. I didn't think I could hope for much smaller than that.

Two full weeks showed no more improvement. Cyrus didn't seem to mind that I couldn't do what he asked, so long as I did something. His number one priority was keeping me alive. Learning control was second.

The glass door hissed closed behind us as we were walking in the chamber at the beginning of another day. "Alright, Terra. You know what to do. Try not to think too hard about it. You were really making progress yesterday."

By progress, he meant that I managed to move a stone without throwing a boulder at him. I shivered trying not to feel my arm throbbing. "I thought you said it would stop hurting," I whispered. I chose a small pebble from the ground to be today's victim.

"It will. I promise it will Terra. Be patient with yourself. Ember was months before she could manipulate fire without getting a migraine."

I moved the stone between my fingers, making no effort to move it just yet. "What about you? You never said where your mark is?"

71

His lips quirked into something of a smile, "On my back. Just about in the middle of my spine. If I over use my powers, I get temporarily paralyzed in the legs."

"And yet you want to fly? Isn't that risky?"

Cyrus shrugged a little. "I'm being careful about it. Like I keep telling you, it's a muscle. You just need to make it stronger. Speaking of which," he made a pointed look at the rock in my hand.

I groaned, wishing I could have kept him in story mode just a little longer. "Fine," I looked down at the rock. Who would have guessed such a tiny thing would cause me so much grief?

The room began to rumble. I clapped a hand over my arm and let the pebble tumble from my fingers. Cyrus picked up another pebble and placed it in my hand. "Focus through your mark. Focus on the pebble and think of it as part of yourself. Just move it. Imagine it flipping over in your hand."

The rumbling got stronger. The boulder next to me cracked in two. "I... I can't... Cyrus, how do I stop it?"

He took the pebble and put a hand on either of my shoulders. "Deep breaths Terra. You need to calm down. Nothing is going to happen. Listen to me."

I sucked in ragged breathes. "O-okay," I tried to imagine nothing happening. That's all I wanted, a calm still nothing. The boulder made a deafening crack that sounded like a gun.

All hell broke loose. A stabbing pain shot through my arm. Pillars of stone burst through the floor. Cyrus jumped away from me, putting his hands out to gain control over the situation. Winds buffeted around the room, toppling the spikes, but he wasn't fast enough. A pillar broke through from right under him. He jumped out of the way but not before the stone tore past his leg.

"Cy-Cyrus!" I ran for him, pillars falling out of my path. "Cyrus oh my god. We need to get you to the med bay." His pants were torn open just above the knee exposing the grated flesh beneath. Blood was oozing from the wound and dripping to the floor.

The winds helped him stand. He reached out and used my shoulder to help him balance. "It's okay Terra. I'm still alive. Help me hop out will you?" His voice was calm, but there was the smallest light of fear in his eyes.

"It's not okay! I almost killed you!" The stones rumbled lightly as we stepped over the threshold of the room. They fell back into silence when we were out.

He winced as he put a little weight on his leg. It seemed he could walk though it was painful. "Occupational hazard Terra. You didn't kill me."

"B-but I..."

"I'll be okay Terra. And this doesn't change anything. We'll just keep trying until you get it."

"Or until I kill you," I corrected. "Pl-please Cyrus. I don't want to hurt anyone."

"You won't. That's why we use the training rooms. You can't hurt anyone so long as you practice in there. The important thing is that you practice."

"Is my life worth the cost of yours?" I already had Grey's life on my hands. I couldn't let anyone else get killed because of me.

"Terra..." Cyrus stopped and turned to me. He was pale but alert. "Do you think that this is the first time something like this has happened? All the trainers are prepared for the worst when they walk in that room with a new recruit. You are very powerful Terra; it'll be harder for you to gain control over that power. You can do it. Just then you made those pillars move out of your way to come get me," He smiled lightly, "your worst enemy is fear. Once you conquer that, you'll be great."

I bit my lip. I wish I could be half as sure as he was.

"You'll see." He looked down then. A small puddle of blood was forming at his foot. "For now, we should really get to the med bay."

The nurses assured Cyrus that his injury was just a deep scrape. There would be quite a scar, but there shouldn't be any lasting effects. I didn't feel any better about it. If he had moved just a second later, it would have been so much worse. My mind replayed the possibilities like the most macabre highlight wheel. How could I ever be of use here when I couldn't do something that I watched even a small boy do? When Ember found out, she didn't blame me. She, like Cyrus, was of the opinion that I would get the hang of it eventually. She was worried about her brother, yes, but she didn't blame me for his injury.

The next day, Cyrus met me in the training room as per normal. I couldn't help but notice the slight bulge of bandages by his knee. A knot formed in my stomach. "How is it?"

Cyrus offered a comforting smile. "Stings a bit when they change the dressing, but other than that fine."

I looked around the room. Someone had cleaned up the blood but just being there made me feel sick. I would have taken double duty with the renovation crew just to not be in that training room.

"You'll get it, Terra," Cyrus must have noticed my expression. "I was thinking we would try physical manipulation again. Sometimes people find that easier. And you did make the arrow head on your first day."

The familiar terror was starting to claw up my throat. My breath caught as the first throb of my arm began. "No. I don't want to today." I tried not to think of the pillars that shot out of the ground the day before. I looked anywhere but at his knee.

"We could try something else then." Cyrus offered. He leaned against one of the boulders. He was putting up a good show but the way he was favouring his good leg... I knew the injury was hurting him.

"No...I don't want to practice today."

"Terra. You can't just not practice. If you don't..."

I shook my head. I backed away to the door hugging my arm. "Not today. It hurts already. I'll do something again..."

"Terra..." Cyrus moved towards me, his hands out. "Come now. If you don't you'll die."

"I said not today!" The boulder closest to my left cracked down the middle. Not wanting to risk it a second longer, I turned on my heel, pulled the door open, and left the room. Cyrus was close on my heels.

"Terra!"

I stopped and turned to face him. His face was drawn into an expression of concern. "I'll practice tomorrow. I can't now. I'll make a mistake again. I know I will. I'll hurt you. Not today. Wait until tomorrow please," I begged.

With a deep sigh, Cyrus nodded. "Just for today. I can't let you go any longer than that without practice. You need to learn the basics."

I managed the ghost of the smile. "Thank you, Cyrus. Thank you," I whispered, before turning and leaving.

Only I didn't train the next day. Or the next either. Cyrus pleaded with me to train but I couldn't bring myself to try. I couldn't step in that room without thinking about the pillars. On the third day, Cyrus asked to see my arm. "The mark is starting to grow again. I know your scared Terra but we really can't put it off any longer. Tomorrow you need to try if you won't today."

"I'll try tomorrow then. I just need more time Cyrus," I pulled my arm back and hurried down the hall.

I decided to go back to the dorms. No one would be there and I would be able to hide for a few hours. I didn't know how I would get out of training tomorrow. Could you fake using your power?

When I turned down the hall, I found that it was not empty. "Merlin!" He was travel worn and his black hair was stuck up at odd angles.

"Oh, hey Terra." Merlin unlocked his door and tossed his rucksack inside, leaving it in an unglorified heap next to his pristinely made bed. "Just got home."

"How was Florida?" He was tanned with the racoon marking of sunglasses around his eyes. He was still wearing the dark brown khaki shorts that he must have put on that morning, with a bomber jacket more suited to the climate above the base.

His smile was blurry and half asleep. "Busy. The mission was successful, though. More or less. The new base is coming along."

"More or less?" I asked with a frown.

"Well, there are always a few who don't take well to it. They knew about the powers but I guess knowing and seeing are very different things."

I nodded, understanding that perfectly well. Here I was thinking up ways to not use my powers, despite knowing perfectly well the consequences.

"Speaking of which, how's your training going?" Merlin asked. He glanced at my arm though it was covered by a long sleeve shirt.

I swore he could read minds. "Good, more or less." I planned on dropping the subject, but when he tilted his head curiously, I sighed. "Not so good. I keep losing control. I almost killed Cyrus. I nearly impaled him and I injured his leg. He says it's okay but..." There was nothing okay about almost mortally wounding somebody. Accident or not.

Looking down at my pent up exterior, Merlin shut the dorm door again. "Come on. I know a good place we can talk about it. And we can grab some oranges from the kitchen on the way. We brought back a whole crate from Florida."

#

It was the first time I got a good look around the mansion above. All other times I was just heading out the front door. It was easy to see that no one walked those halls anymore. I caught glimpses of the

76

ghostly rooms as Merlin led me towards the stairs. Thin streams of light filtered through thick brocade curtains, falling on the fine layer of dust clinging to the dark wood floors. Whatever furniture remained was covered by thick white sheets. The crystal chandeliers, that must have once glimmered in the morning sunlight, were dull and hung with cobwebs.

"Most of the place is like this. It's a shame. It really must have been something," Merlin said, reading my thoughts.

"You really don't use any of it?"

"The ballroom from time to time. Not in months though."

The rococo staircase twisted up to the second level. "Where are you taking me, Merlin?" I asked as we stepped out onto the landing.

Rather than answering, he flashed me one of his easy sunny smiles and pushed open the first set of carved wooden doors.

The room was breath-taking. Glass walls looked over a forest of vibrant green, glowing gold, and fiery red leaves. The morning sun was streaming in, feeding the herbs and flowers growing in the planter boxes at the windows edge.

Merlin pulled the sheet off a wicker settee and gestured for me to sit. "Tell me your woes."

I sighed and sat, rolling my orange between my hands. "I'm going to kill Cyrus if I keep this up. I just know it."

Merlin made a noise in the back of his throat that sounded somewhere in between 'I know' and 'I see'. "And, what does Cyrus think?" He sat down next to me and peeled his orange, brightening the air with the sweet tang of citrus.

"He insists that I'm not going to kill him and what I did to his leg is just a scratch. I saw it. It's bigger than my hand. That is not a scratch."

"Well you know, he is your trainer." Merlin teased, and popped a piece of orange in his mouth, "Occupational hazard and all that. Besides, if he thought you were actually going to kill him, I think he would be a little less, shall we say, optimistic?"

I rolled my eyes, "You know that's the same thing he said," I looked up at him. "What was it like for you when you started?"

Merlin blinked. "Me?" He scratched his head, "Well, I can't, actually remember precisely. Um, I sort of... accidentally drowned myself. According to my trainer, I was doing really well at first, making little fountains and whatnot. So I popped down one day for a little extra training and got in way over my head," He offered a sheepish smile. "I was trying to figure out how to breath underwater. So I made a sphere and put it around my head and- well I panicked. Couldn't figure out how to get the thing off. I ran out of air eventually and collapsed. Thankfully there's only an inch of water in the room or else I might have actually drowned. But I hit my head something awful. Still have the scar, see," Merlin turned and pushed up a bit of hair just back from his left temple. "It did some funny things to my memory. But I didn't try things like that by myself anymore."

I was shocked. Merlin seemed so secure with his power. Or at least, the little I saw of it. "Weren't you scared to try again?"

"Yeah well, it was either do it or die. I rather like being solid. So, I managed to swallow the fear. Between the two, I'm more scared of Telluria killing me, then accidentally killing myself," His eyes darkened. "I had a little sister. Her name was Celeste. She was water like me. It was before the cure was made. I was there with her at the end."

I looked up at him through my lashes. There was an ache in his voice that I recognized.

"She would have liked having magical powers. It was what kept me going. She was only little when she died, but she had the fury of a hurricane sometimes. I had no doubt she would have called me a dummy for giving up."

I pulled my legs up on the settee with me. "Grey would have said I was being an idiot," I muttered, though smiled a little. "Though he would have been as scared as I am. We did all the big stuff together. This...is really the first time I've done anything this big by myself."

78

"Maybe Grey can be your Celeste?" Merlin suggested. "You can't hurt him, Terra," There was a gentleness in his voice that told me he wasn't saying it to hurt me. After all, he was the only one who knew the whole story.

I bit my lip. "It's worth a try I guess," I glanced at my arm. The mark was starting to grow again. "Besides if I skip any more training sessions, Cyrus might just get desperate."

The easy grin drifted back on Merlin's face. "He just might. Don't be too hard on him, his heart is in the right place." He then reached over poked my orange. "If you just keep playing with that I'm going to eat it."

In spite of myself, I giggled. "Famished are you?" I peeled the orange and handed him a wedge of it.

"I didn't risk life and liberty for the oranges to go to waste."

\#

I wish I could have said it was the pain that woke me. There was no pain, just a stone hand. The numbness spread up into my shoulder. I just stared at it. My whole body was frozen in the undeniable truth that my left hand up to as far as my elbow was solid stone.

Then the panic came, thick and clawing like glue and knives. I sucked in shattered breathes, my lungs refusing to register the oxygen.

I threw back the blankets and half ran, half crept to our bathroom. I closed the door as quietly as I could, which still managed to sound thunderous.

This wasn't supposed to be happening. The training was meant to be a cure, to halt the lines from spreading. The training worked, but I hadn't gone in days.

I turned on the water in the sink. How could I have let it get this far? They warned me. I knew this would happen. But at the idea of using my power, my stomach churned.

I couldn't breathe. I couldn't think. I grabbed the luffa from the shower and started scrubbing my arm. "Please...Please..." Sand flaked off. I turned on the water and held my arm under the flow. Hoping, preying, I willed the stone to crumble away like caked-on-mud and reveal bare flesh beneath. The stone was unrelenting as rivulets of water channelled through the fine fissures.

"No...No...please. Please come off. Please. Please!" The luffa thrown aside, I scraped at the stone with my bare hand. My fingernails chipping, more flecks of sand rattled to the floor until finally I tore off a sizeable chunk. I lifted my stone arm in some vain hope to see skin beneath. Fresh blood pooled to the surface mixing with the water and ran down my arm.

I bit back the fresh sob clawing at my throat. My grip slipping from my will to keep the situation under control, I started slamming my arm against the sink. Porcelain shattered and I felt nothing. "GET IT OFF! GET IT OFF!"

"Terra? Terra, what's wrong?"

I froze. The door clicked against the lock and I tasted bile. "N-nothing. J-just go back to sleep."

I could almost picture Ember on the other side. Hands on her hips to match the sigh of worry mixed with exasperation. "Terra. One does not simply scream 'get it off' over nothing. I'm coming in." There was no time to react. Before I could even contemplate blocking the door, Ember burst through. I didn't notice at the time, but the metal of the lock was glowing red and trickling down the side of the door frame.

My only defence from this intrusion was to angle my arm away from her. "It's nothing really. Just go."

One swift look over my shoulder at the broken and bloody sink and Ember grabbed me. I pushed my arm further behind my back but she noticed. Taking a hold of my bad shoulder, she hauled my arm forward. Once again I felt a stab of that clawing feeling in my throat to make up for the lack of feeling in my arm. "Oh. My. God." Without any further comment, she stepped aside and pushed me from the room and out into the hallway.

80

The barrage of fluorescent lights stung my eyes. "I am going to kill Cy," Ember sounded like she was on a battle march. With a fury like Ember's, that was a near possibility. "How in the name of Hellfire did he let this happen. I am going to kill Cy."

"It wasn't his fault," I murmured, my own voice sounding like a croak. "If I had listened..."

My protests fell on deaf ears. We reached Cyrus' and Merlin's door. Not willing to risk letting go of me, Ember held my arm in a vice like grip while her other fist pounded on the door. "Cyrus Marcus Chiaro!"

Ember kept pounding until a very irritated and sleepy looking Cyrus opened the door. "Wha...what time is it?" From the doorway, I would see Merlin as well, sitting up in bed and rubbing his eyes.

"Get dressed. You need to take Terra down to the training room immediately. Look at her arm," Ember pulled me forward and brandished my stone appendage.

Cyrus took my offered arm in his hands. "Wow..." He stated with a sort of bland awe. He looked from my arm to my face and I knew what he would see there. I was pale and drained with wide darting eyes. I had no delusion that he couldn't feel me shaking either.

Cyrus dropped my arm and turned back into the room. In quick succession he pulled on a shirt, not bothering to change out of his pyjama bottoms, and put on shoes. Merlin followed suit. Ready, Cyrus swept past and led the way. Seeing no way out, I followed. A hand slipped into mine and I looked to my right to see Merlin. He offered a small half grin that didn't quite meet his eyes. "You'll be alright Terra. Just do what Cyrus says. You aren't his first slip."

I bit my lip and nodded. Unable to speak, I just squeezed his hand back.

#

At this time of night, the passages were mostly clear. We passed a couple night guards, but that was all. Cyrus marched me directly into our usual training room. The earth and stone surroundings

81

were both welcoming and looming. Cyrus picked up a small pebble and placed it in my stone palm. I winced at the sound. "Move it," he ordered.

I looked down at it. My stone arm was being propped up by my flesh one. I tried to focus, the familiar beat of the earth's pulse rising in my wrist. It ricocheted until my whole body was trembling so bad that the pebble simply slid from my hand.

"Again," a gust of wind dropped a fresh pebble in my palm. Again it slipped before my power could even take root.

"Terra..." Ember stood with her arms wrapped around herself at the side of the room. Next to her was Merlin, standing tall and straight with his arms by his sides. There was the slightest crease in his brows.

Another stone, and another drop. The gust of wind did not bring another stone. Instead, I was I was buffeted and sent stumbling towards the wall. My stone arm landed against the wall and the sound of crashing rocks echoed through the small room. I could taste blood in my mouth. I looked down and saw that the wound amid the fissures had reopened and blood was trickling down my fingertips.

"Did you think we were kidding?" Cyrus demanded, rocking me with another gust of wind. In that moment, there was no question who his father was. "This is what happens Terra when you don't use your powers. It's your arm today. It will keep going. Tomorrow it'll spread to your torso. Another couple days it'll be your legs. In a week you'll be in a shell of stone, locked in as your organs are taken one by one. Is that what you want Terra?"

"N-no. But I..."

"There are no buts. You do this, or you die. You were told this at the very beginning. And now, you see the truth of it. This isn't a game. It isn't like school where you can just keep trying until you get it. You need to do this now. You are sick, and that sickness is going to kill you."

I pushed off the wall and took a step towards the middle of the room again. I could, I know that I could. I already did it before. It was just the fear of the act itself that was stopping me. I tried to focus on that if nothing else. I needed to. It was just medicine. That was all. Though the memory of me nearly killing Cyrus came fast and clear to the front of my mind.

Cyrus picked up another stone and came over to place it in my palm. "Come on. I don't care if you try to bury me under a mountain. You need to do this now."

I nodded. "Okay," and looked down at the stone. Beat. Beat. Beat. Earth's hum rumbled under my own heartbeat and the muted drip of my blood to the floor. I looked up at Cyrus, then to Ember, and to Merlin. Absolute trust in every one of their faces, neither looked the least concerned that I might do something horribly wrong any second now. I took a breath, trying to concentrate on everything around me. Focusing on that familiar deep beat of something far older then all of us.

The stone moved, just the tiniest rattle in place. Another beat more, and it rolled over and fell off my hand. I knew I couldn't stop. If I stopped the fear would come back. I followed the beats. Sinking to my knees I picked up a handful of pebbles and let them trickle through my fingers. The first few fell as they were. But then they started to crumble, disintegrating to sand. I kept this going, working through one handful at a time until I was surrounded by a very small section of dessert. From there I worked backwards. Running my fingers through the sand, making them clump and turn to smooth pebbles once again.

Like working a rarely used muscle, I was tiring quickly. Small beads of sweat were forming on my brow. The room was absolutely silent but for the rattle of pebbles, and my laboured breathing.

"Terra... you're using both hands." Merlin sunk down beside me, touching my left wrist.

So lost in focus I hadn't noticed the stone starting to give way to flesh. My fingers were raw and pink. Thin lines of stone wrapping around them like so many rings. My forearm was still solid.

"Keep going. Just a little more." He lifted up another handful of sand for me and let it fall into my open palms. I merged these together, feeling the solid mass start act like clay under my hands. My breathing was starting to run ragged as I pulled one edge of the stone to create a point. I picked up another handful and did the same. It wasn't until I built a small wall to connect the two points that I realized I was building a castle. It was ike the sand castles me and Grey would make as kids, just more solid.

Catching on to what I was doing, Merlin drew a line around the forming structure. A thin stream of water created a mote. I added a drawbridge and finished the walls. I wanted to add more, but by then I was struggling for each breath. I looked down at my arm again. Only a small band remained around my wrist, with the familiar tendrils twisting from finger to elbow. I looked up at Merlin and could only manage a small exhausted smile.

"That will do for now. You did good Terra," Cyrus murmured, standing to the side of the room with Ember. A small smile on his own face. "Go rest. Do you know where your scheduled for tomorrow afternoon?"

"Med bay," I answered, looking up at the siblings. Ember was grinning like a Cheshire cat.

"I'll have a chat with them. Let them know that I want you to have an extra training session with me then. You get the morning off to rest." He nodded to Merlin then, "Merlin, think you could tend to that arm?" It was still pretty raw looking, though the bleeding had stopped.

"Sure thing," Merlin answered, standing and offering a hand to me. I took it and got to my feet. "Come on Miss. Off to the med bay with you. Er...what time is it?"

Ember glanced out the window to the clock in the hall. "6:30. Might as well get breakfast once you're done then. We'll see you there?"

I paused, feeling completely drained. I wasn't sure I would stay awake as far as the med bay let alone breakfast. "I'll see you at lunch. I'd rather not fall headfirst into my oatmeal."

84

CHAPTER SEVEN

Choices

It was on that night I found my strength. I had stepped back from the brink of no return and could only get better. Cyrus had me focus on sculpting things. It didn't matter what; sandcastles, pillars, or just large rocks. Soon I could build elaborate structures without tiring so easily. By that point, Cyrus started offering resistance. It turned into a game between us; I would build, and he would knock down. When we started this game, he won almost all the time. In time, I realized that it was sheer force of will that gave your conjuring its strength. Cyrus' at first was stronger than mine, but as the weeks went on his winds were as effective as the wind through the mountains. Sometimes small chips would flake away but the main structure stood strong.

I was there for six months. It didn't feel like that long as every day I was busy from sunrise to set; every morning I was training with Cyrus. As I got better, I didn't need to practice for full mornings anymore, an hour or two was usually enough. I started using the extra time to catch up on work or to simply help out where I was needed. My favourite place was usually the library. The recruitment team were almost always doing research their in-between missions.

What I did after lunch depended on schedule. There were days I was in the offices, keeping things organized or helping the recruitment team. Some days I was in the vehicle hanger. I knew nothing about motors but recognized most tools and I could do basic things on my own. Some of my favourite days were spent in the greenhouse and solarium. There, more than any other department, I saw the good our powers could do. Fire types kept the gardens warm,

85

whilst air, water, and earth gave the plants a strength in which they could even grow in the midst of winter. I got to spend even more time there after I kicked out of the kitchen for burning an entire batch of oats. The remaining place where I spent the most of my time was in the med bay. The medical knowledge I picked up was rudimentary at best, but I found I was good with people. Usually when I delivered meals, medication, or changed dressings, I stopped to talk for a few minutes. The vast majority of those who came through med bay were new recruits. Most were confused and bewildered like I was at first. I did what I could to make the transition easier for them: answering questions, telling my story, or asking them about theirs.

Six months marked the time when I would have to choose a speciality within the rebellion. I had six months to experience all that I could so that when this day came, I would know where I belonged. Or...I could leave if that was my choice.

That morning, Ember was acting more mischievous than normal. I was used to this by now after living with her for this long. Even so, I went through my morning routine with more caution than usual, double and triple checking everything for a possible prank before using it. Strangely though, nothing was set up.

"Ready for breakfast?" Ember was chipper as if she already had her rare morning coffee. She was dressed and sitting on her bed waiting for me when I came out of our shared bathroom.

"Yeah just give me a minute," I grabbed my brush and pulled it through my hair a few times before turning for the door. "Okay, let's go."

Cyrus and Merlin were already tucking into breakfast at our usual table when we came into the dining hall. Ember and I went up to the front to get ours before joining them.

"Nervous about today?" Merlin grinned at me over his plate of eggs and toast.

"A bit. Can't say I've been feeling too stellar about any of my jobs," I admitted. Marcus had the reports from all of the departments. The department heads could make recommendations, but ultimately he would decide your fate. I didn't feel like I was made for any job in particular. Not in the same way, Ember, Cyrus, or Merlin all seemed made for theirs. Ember was playing with springs and gears since she could grasp objects in her hands. Cyrus had helped his sister with her powers and even figured out some tricks to help Marcus. He was good at finding out what made a person's power tick. As for Merlin, he was good with people. His enthusiasm for the rebellion was infectious, and he had the charisma to be on first name terms with almost anyone he met. Not to mention, he hated being cooped up in the underground complex and lived to get back out into the outside world.

Merlin patted my shoulder sympathetically, "Don't worry. That oatmeal wasn't so bad- Ow!"

I had punched him in the arm. "Marcus isn't going to make me a cook! He doesn't want food poisoning."

Cyrus was chuckling. "No one knows where they are going to fit. It's why management watches you so closely. They can usually see aptitude even if you can't."

I remembered Cyrus saying that he had to give a report on my skill with my powers. I suddenly wondered what he added to my file

"And besides, if you really don't like what they choose, you can request a transfer. It happens," he continued.

The playful banter was quickly cascading into real nerves. My toast tasted like sawdust. "They've never kicked anyone out before...have they? For not fitting any role?"

"Oh yeah. All the time. They send you to live as a troll under the Golden Gate Bridge," Merlin had a large bite of toast, chewing thoughtfully as I stared at him in mock horror. His face lit with a half-smile. "Don't worry about it. They've probably had something picked for months. They just wait till six to be super sure. Well, that and..."

All three of them fell silent, my face felt hot. My original contract was up. I could leave today if I wanted to. I knew that I was better equipt to survive on my own. Honestly, I didn't know what I wanted to do. My friends kept asking me, but I could never commit to an answer.

Somehow I hadn't noticed Ember sneaking off but I noticed her come back. She carried a stack of tiny pancakes on a tea saucer. As she set it down in front of me, a single flame hovered just over the stack. "Happy six months to you! Happy six months to you! Happy six months to Terra! Happy six months to you!" Ember did not sing well but the effort she went through touched my heart.

I hugged her fiercely, "Thanks, Em," I whispered, my voice getting thick. As I pulled away I arranged my face into what I hoped was a smile, and blew out the flame. I gave each of them one of the small pancakes.

"Whether you stay or go, we just wanted to give you a good sending off." Ember was like a wick drowning in wax; burning bright, but dimming. They were all used to newbies coming and going, never knowing if they would see new friends again after the sixth month.

After breakfast, as we got up to go, Ember embraced me again. "Good luck. And remember, the bed is always yours."

Cyrus put a hand on my shoulder. "You're alright Terra. If you stay, I know you'll do good here."

Finally, Merlin. He didn't say anything at first just nodded towards the exit. "Come on, I'm going by that way anyway. I'll walk you," his hand slid around mine as we left together.

It was silence until we made it to Marcus's office door. He would be expecting me. My heart was beating in my throat. I yearned for home, a place I could never go. Or maybe I was home.

Merlin stopped me before going in. When I turned to face him, he was looking at his shoes. "Hey ah... I just wanted to say... I hope you stay. But... if you go, I'll be in touch."

My brows knitted. "I thought I wasn't allowed to contact anyone once I left?" Almost immediately I regretted my choice of words. "If I left."

"Well... you can't. Not officially, but I'm out there all the time. There're no rules about us just happening to run into each other," The familiar hopeful light filled his grey-blue eyes. "But hey... if you do go, I just wanted to give you this. To remind you."

He took something out of his pocket and held it out in his open palm. It was a pendant of raw jade hanging from a leather cord. The stone was tumbled and polished to a shine.

"Found it. I thought it would match your eyes," he looked up at me and slipped the necklace over my head.

"Merlin, it's beautiful. Thank you," I whispered, touching the smooth jade, "but I didn't need this to remember you. Or Ember. Or Cyrus."

He rubbed the back of his neck and dropped his gaze to the floor. "Well...Marcus is waiting. Better let you go."

He turned to leave. I reached for his arm. "Merlin..."

"Yeah?"

I leaned up and kissed his cheek. "You're right. I do like it here. See you around."

I turned and walked into Marcus' office.

#

Marcus was waiting at his desk. It was an industrial piece of furniture of faded green. It matched the rest of the office, dated but functional and organized. Marcus was not the type to have a cascading pile of papers all over his desk. At the moment, the only thing in front of him was a single manila folder.

"Please, sit," he gestured to the chair across from him.

I sat, my mouth too dry to attempt talking just yet. Part of me just wanted to sink through the floor and disappear.

Marcus opening the folder and brought up the topmost page to read aloud, "Terra Chase. You've been with us for six months. This marks the end of our original agreement. You have received adequate training to survive with Telluria on your own. We have received in return, your services to the rebellion," he looked over the paper at me, "I'm sure you're wondering how it is we usually proceed from here?"

I only nodded.

He swept a hand over the small stack of papers. "This is your profile. Six months' worth of data on your work within the various departments. You can look at it later if you like." Marcus made the attempt of a smile, just enough for it to touch his eyes before letting it fade. "Normally, we will start with me telling you what your results are; where your strengths and weaknesses lie. I will then tell you what job I believe you are best suited for should you chose to remain with us."

"And if I don't?" I whispered.

"If it is your desire to leave, I will personally escort you to your room so that you may gather your things. Our pilot will take you wherever you want to start your new life. I word of caution, however, pick someplace where you can speak the language."

I realized, after a silent moment, that this was Marcus's attempt at humour. I was too bundled up to properly recognize it at the time. "I don't know what I want to do yet."

Marcus nodded, "Not uncommon. Let us get started shall we." He picked up the first paper again. "Terra...personally profile; level-headed, a good problem solver, good with people, irrational when frightened, stubborn. Sound about right?"

I became very interested in my shoes. Again, I nodded.

"Mm... indeed. Next, medical bay. Good bedside manner. You have little aptitude for healing, but you are adequate in first aid. Much the same with your time in the workshop and construction, a basic grasp of the skills," He sifted through the papers, lifting the department reports one by one. "I have a glowing recommendation here from the director of the greenhouses. And recruitment says that you were a valuable help in their preparations for the past two missions," turning to the last page, Marcus's mouth twitched like he was holding back a laugh. "The kitchen... not that burnt oatmeal ever harmed anyone, but I don't think you'll make a chef Miss Chase."

I sunk down in my chair a little, but despite that, I felt the corners of my lips quirking up.

Marcus put the papers down, closed the folder, and folded his hands on top of his desk, "Cyrus says you are a strong elementalist. Despite your, shall we say rocky start?" He looked up at me, if not a little shrewdly. "After you got over your initial hurdle, you've grown quite talented. I must ask... what do you think of your powers now?"

I didn't expect to be asked anything, I floundered a little. "I was terrified at first. But... it got easier once I accepted that not using them will kill me. The mark is as small as it's ever been." I folded my hands neatly in my lap, "I'm enjoying them now. Your son is an excellent teacher."

"Good good," Marcus made a small noise in his throat. "I've been told that you spend a lot of time with the newer recruits as well. You've accompanied Merlin in orientation, and you've helped some of the more uncertain recruits through the first few days of training."

"It was really Merlin's idea. He thought they would be able to relate to me more," someone else who was scared and alone and unsure not long ago. "I know my transition into this world was less than graceful. I wanted to help make it easier for others."

"Merlin's idea or not, not everyone can calm the newly sick. When they first come to us, they are frightened and often irrational. Many believe they are going to die. A person with no hope is a very dangerous thing."

It was hard to believe that I was one of those people just months ago. When I ran through the woods from home, I thought I only had months, maybe weeks to live before Telluria ended me. There was a resolve that came with the realization of your own absolution.

"If you choose to stay, your assignment will be to join the recruitment team. I want you to continue to work with the new recruits. Additionally, you'll be joining the rest of the team on extraction missions into the cities. We need to save as many as we can from New Atlantis."

My mouth hung open a little. Recruitment? Of all jobs I might have been expecting, that certainly wasn't one of them. I would be working with Merlin and the rest of the team. I didn't know what to say.

"It is your choice, Terra. Stay, and take your place bringing more to our cause. Or, if you still want to go, I wish you luck in your new life. You may not, however, leave this office until a decision is made. Take your time."

Marcus stood up from his desk. The legs of the chair scraped against the hard tiled floor. He picked up my folder and handed it to me on his way out. "You may read this as well."

My hands were trembling, clutching the manila folder like a lifeline. Stay or go, it seemed like such a simple choice. Two lives stretched out before me. One was wild, uncertain, but free. The other was structured, detailed, but meaningful.

If I left, I would be free of all of this: no more training, no more pseudo-military rules, I would be free. I could start a life all my own, somewhere far away from anyone who ever knew me.

And yet, I would always have the mark. I would always have to hide. I didn't want to stop and consider Merlin, Cyrus, and Ember. I would never see them again. I know Merlin said he would keep in touch, but we both knew that would be impossible.

My eyes fell on the bracelet Grey gave me. That seemed like another lifetime ago. What would he think? The Grey I grew up with would have wanted to leave but the Grey that had made me run on the last night of his life, he was someone else. That Grey would have done anything to stop New Atlantis from hurting more people in the name of a cure. Grey's spirit carried me to a decision.

Marcus returned roughly an hour later. He carried two mugs of steaming coffee. The folder was still clutched in my hands. "I made a decision."

Marcus set down the cups and turned to face me.

"I want to stay," I looked up at him, and for perhaps the first time in Marcus's presence, I smiled.

As did he. Marcus handed me one of the cups, and raised his own, "May I be the first to welcome you," he stated and drank.

#

Nothing is official without paperwork. Marcus had a small stack of forms for me to fill out. My pen hovered over a section regarding next of kin. "If my parents were both cured, will they even care?" I asked softly.

"The compulsion is the only reason they are still able to care," Marcus reminded me, not unkindly. "Otherwise, instead of simply reporting you to New Atlantis, they would likely tear you to shreds."

I filled out their information and slid the forms back to him. "Have you heard anything about them? My parents?"

Marcus sipped the final dregs of his coffee. "They have stopped searching for you. Officially you have been declared dead."

"Oh," I didn't know what I was hoping for but that wasn't it. "What about Mrs McNair?"

Marcus shook his head. "We have not been able to contact her. I can assure you however that New Atlantis has left her alone."

I hoped that my parents were still inviting her over for supper and Dad's homemade wine. I hated the idea of her being alone. "What now?"

"The recruitment director, Josh, is expecting you. He'll be in the main recruitment office. If not, try the library."

#

I hoped to run into Merlin, Ember, or Cyrus on the way, but it was mid-morning and the halls were empty. The recruitment office was just down the hall from Marcus's office.

The office was bigger than Marcus' but only because it was usually used by several people at once. It had a desk and a table with several chairs. The table was strewn with books and papers while almost every spare inch of wall space was plastered with mission details.

At the moment, there was only one person in the office. "Terra! Marcus said you would be along," Josh beamed at me. He was good-natured and easily one of the tallest people in the rebellion. He didn't have a visible mark but I knew him to be water type. "I'm so glad you agreed to join us. You're wonderful with the new recruits, I was so worried we were going to lose you."

"What can I say. This place has grown on me. Though I do miss windows now and then." I replied with a shrug.

"You'll have no lack of the great outdoors with us I assure you," Josh clapped me on the shoulder and directed me further inside. "You couldn't have picked a better time to join recruitment. We're planning to go to Quebec City in a couple weeks. I wish I had a little more time to get you prepared, but I'm sure you'll be splendid."

"Don't they speak French there?" I didn't know any French. Aside from 'bonjour', and 'je ne parle pas francais'.

Josh tilted his hand back and forth. "Half and half. The uncured locals prefer French. But New Atlantis operates in English, and as such, the cured do as well. Language won't be a problem."

We walked further into the room, and I scanned the papers over the back wall "So why there?" I asked, curious about the choice. The photos showed a picturesque city with basilicas and tall narrow homes on a cobbled road.

Josh pointed to a photograph of a castle on a hill. "Chateau Frontenac. It was a hotel once, but it's fallen into disuse. There have been some rumours of squatters."

At once I understood. "Interesting to have squatters when New Atlantis gives everyone housing," I murmured. "Do you think they're all sick? How many?"

Josh shrugged. "We don't know. It's just rumours. But hopefully, we'll find a few there."

#

After talking about the mission, Josh got to explaining what would be expected of me as a member of the recruitment team. There were skills that I would need to brush up on, rudimentary French for example. But now that I wouldn't be working in the other departments, I had plenty of time to catch up.

When I asked Josh where the rest of the team were, he said they were all in the library. He had planned to have them come to the office to welcome me to the team properly until he realized the time.

"Not to worry. Meet back here after lunch. Everyone can find out the good news then."

I was practically skipping back to the dining hall with the realization that Ember, Cyrus, and Merlin had gone the entire morning without hearing from me. Would they think I had left?

The dining hall was just starting to fill when I got there. I hurried to get my serving of minestrone soup and made my way back to our regular table.

None of the others were at the table yet, but it didn't take long before my ears filled with the expected excited squeal.

"Oh my god oh my god oh my god! I knew you would stay!"

I turned in my seat to let Ember tackle me. "I stayed," I affirmed once Ember had let me go.

"Good to see you, Terra," Cyrus sat down across from me. He was windswept and smiling brightly like the sun.

"How could I leave you guys? Really?" The fact that I had considered leaving was behind me.

"What's your assignment?" Ember asked, bubbling with questions.

Before I could answer, Merlin joined us. The moment he saw me, his face eased into a relieved smile. "I didn't see you come in. I got a bit worried."

I flipped my hair over my shoulder. "Well, maybe next time pull your head out of the books a little faster."

"Yeah, well- How did you know that's what I was doing?" Merlin tilted his head.

My heart thumped uncomfortably in my chest. He reminded me of a puppy. "Our superior told me. You know... Josh."

"Josh? You mean- No way! Oh man, that's awesome!" Merlin punched the air, suddenly grinning like Cheshire.

"What's awesome? Care to fill me and my sister in there Merlin?" Cyrus asked over his soup.

"I'm on the recruitment team," I explained. "I'll be working with Merlin." I turned back to Merlin. "And I'll be going on the Quebec mission too."

"Sa-weet! See I knew you were cut out for this. This is just too awesome. We need to celebrate!"

"Eat first. You still have work to do," Cyrus chuckled and gestured from Merlin to his bowl. He then looked to me. "That's great to hear Terra. I know father made the right choice. Just... try not to let Merlin get too crazy 'kay?"

I giggled. Beside me, Merlin and Ember were planning a party. "I'll take good care of him. Promise."

CHAPTER EIGHT

Storming the Castle

The recruitment team was a small, tight-knit group. As Josh kept telling me, within the base we were safe, we were well fed, everything was under control. Out in the world, New Atlantis had the control. Those of us in the recruitment team needed to know that we could trust each other no matter what happened. Josh admitted to being picky, and that Marcus wouldn't assign someone to the recruitment team without Josh's blessing.

It was a very strange job. While in the base, our time was split between research and physical conditioning. Josh was a firm believer that you couldn't be too prepared. In ideal situations, he wanted us to know everything about a city before we left. He wanted us to be familiar with the streets, the customs and, in some cases, even a beginner's grasp of the local language.

The physical training, we almost always did together. The only exception being that not everyone was afflicted with Telluria. Four members of the recruitment team; Tasha, Braxton, Simon, and Edgar were sympathetic to the cause. They trained with traditional weapons while Josh, Elleen, Merlin, Kalle, Frank and I trained with our elements. Working in groups, we were able to experiment with how the elements worked together. Every day we went for runs in the woods around the base. We were usually jumping, climbing, and scurrying along like a group of overly energetic squirrels. It was the happiest I had been since Grey's death.

Two weeks went by too fast. Everything was prepared; our supplies were gathered and loaded into the resistance plane. I had even gained a tiny vocabulary of French to appease the uncured locals. Still, in such short a time, I couldn't be sure if I was ready with any certainty. Merlin was confident that I would be fine.

On the morning of departure, I was up at the crack of dawn. I was dressed ready for a Canadian spring; faded jeans, a white t-shirt, my old hoodie, and a rain jacket. I tackled my hair into twin braids. As time ticked ever closer I fidgeted with whatever I could get my hands on. Ember watched me with some amusement, "You'll be fine Terra. You survived weeks out in the world by yourself. This time, you'll be with a team and you have your element for defence. You'll be safe as kittens."

"Are kittens a relatively safe thing? Last I checked their cute little fuzzy faces distracted you from their claws."

Ember flung her hands up in exasperation, "Safe as a hamster then." She put her hands on my shoulders, "You'll do fine. Remember your umbrella? Ça va?"

I sighed, "Ça va bien, merci," I murmured. "And I should get going, I guess... au revoir?"

"Goodbye seems a little final. I'll see you when you get back," Ember gathered me up in a vice-like hug, "take care of yourself."

#

The rest of the team were supposed to be meeting in the vehicle hanger. I had hoped to see Merlin in the hallway but he must have left before me. The halls were empty and there was no sound of movement coming from his room. Pity, his easy-going nature would have calmed my nerves a little.

As I walked through the hanger, I found that the plane had been moved outside. I stepped out of the small side access door into the cool glowing dawn. I was the last to arrive. Everyone else was already gathered around the plane. It was a small private jet that once belonged to the owner of the mansion above. For years, it had sat in disuse until a pilot joined the resistance. Merlin looked up at me as I approached and waved, his black hair a slept-in mess on the top of his head. A man I didn't recognize was chatting with Josh next to our mode of transportation.

Josh clapped his hands together when he noticed I had joined the group, "Ah good that's everyone. Just in time. Everything ready Arthur?"

The man I didn't know, Arthur the pilot, nodded. "She's ready when you are."

I leaned over to Merlin as the pilot opened the side door of the plane. "Remind me again how New Atlantis won't be suspicious about an unauthorized plane in the Quebec City airspace?"

As if sensing my nerves, Merlin patted my arm. "For one, they would have to physically see us. We won't show up on any of their radar. That, and if they do try to contact us, Arthur knows what to say."

I tried to feel as secure as Merlin looked and climbed up the few stairs into the plane. I made a beeline for a window seat of ivory leather, feeling that not being able to see the ground would be much like being blindfolded.

Merlin sat down in the seat that faced mine with a small folding table between us. His lips quirked in a half smile. "Nervous?"

I raised an eyebrow at him, forcing what I hoped was a look of bravado. The effect was shattered slightly by the hum of engines coming to life. "Should I be? I chose this remember."

"It is your first time," He reminded me though smiling. "First time flying too?"

The engine was getting louder. I nodded feeling my mouth go dry. "It's not that far. Why couldn't we have just driven there?"

Merlin sighed softly. "Because it's weirder to see a random van on the highway, then to notice a plane in the air," He reminded me again.

I knew that. I understood it all perfectly. The plane lurched, and I gave a little squeak. My hands clenched on the handles of the seat.

"Hey," Merlin reached across to me, touching my hand. My knuckles were turning white, "scared of flying?"

"I don't like leaving the ground," I corrected him. Maybe it was just the earth elemental in me talking, but I would have preferred to leave the flying to Cyrus.

I looked out the window. We were lined up with the runway, the engines were roaring in my ears and I felt the rumble of wheels beneath us.

"Why don't you tell me about your family? You said your dad was a botanist before the outbreak?"

I tore my eyes away from the window. "I... yeah. He... he worked in genetics. The university where he worked was trying to create crops that would grow in the most hostile environments."

"How did that go?" Merlin asked, somehow completely uninterested by the sensation of the wheels leaving the ground.

I dared a look out the window and regretted it immediately. The landscape was flying by and falling away from us at a dizzying speed. I closed my eyes, "They were aiming for a crop that could grow anywhere. One that had the genes to survive the desert, and the Arctic, and the moon. Given enough water and sunlight anyway." The plane lurched in a touch of turbulence, I gripped the chair tighter, "They didn't get it down to one seed. But they did have four different strands that did well in their prospective target zones. Dad's favourites were the water seeds. You could throw them into any water and they would grow right there on the surface. Saltwater worked best."

Merlin's face lit up, "Ocean farming huh? I like the sound of that."

"Of course you would," I rolled my eyes, in spite of the plane steadily rising into the clouds.

"Why didn't it become a thing, though? Something like that sounds useful."

100

I sighed, remembering Dad's disheartened face whenever he told me the story, "A lot of the university was damaged in the riots. There wasn't much that survived. He's not sure if any seeds are still around, or who has them." There was a dull ache in my chest. I would love to see Dad again, to hear him chatter about plants with the enthusiasm of a toddler talking about toys. "He still has most of the research. Before I left, he had put in a request to continue his work. I wonder if he ever heard back," my voice trailed off.

Merlin gave my hand a little squeeze, "If he did, we can probably find out. If you'd like?"

My eyes softened and I turned my hand to lace my fingers through his. "Thanks. I'd like that."

Overhead, there was a soft dinging sound. Merlin let go of my hand and undid his seatbelt.

"What are you doing? Should you be walking around?" I asked, having a dizzying waking nightmare of him being tossed into a wall next time we hit turbulence.

"I'll be just a second. Don't worry," Merlin chuckled, and walked to the front of the plane. Just before the door to the cockpit, there was a metal cabinet. I had assumed it was filled with parachutes in case the engines failed and we all needed to jump. Merlin opened one of the bottom doors and pulled out a battered blue box before returning to me.

He set the box down on the table between us before sitting and buckling himself back in, much to my relief. "One thousand glorious pieces of a train running through the mountains. That should keep your mind off proximity to the ground."

I almost laughed, "A puzzle? Really?"

"Eh well, it was this or chess. And my chess game isn't so strong." Merlin opened the box and began sorting out edge pieces.

"I never learned chess," I mused as I too started to sort through the jagged pieces.

Merlin tilted his head, "Well, in that case, I'll teach you on the flight back. Oh, look a corner piece."

I chanced a look out the window again. Through the clouds, I could see patches of green miles and miles below us. It would have been beautiful if it weren't so surreal.

"Don't worry," Merlin's voice had turned gentle again, "You're not so far from the earth. You have a little piece right there," He pointed at my necklace with its pendant of polished jade.

I touched it lightly, feeling the cool smooth stone beneath my fingers. It hummed under my touch almost like something alive. "I didn't think of that."

"If you always wear it, you won't need to be scared of leaving the ground. You'll always have a little piece with you." Merlin touched my hand again, just a light brush against my fingers, "That and puzzles to keep your mind off it all. Come on, I have my doubts if we'll get it done.

#

We did, in fact, finish the puzzle but only because Frank and Kalle helped us. Josh and Elleen had opted for the chess board, and by the sounds of things, Elleen was winning.

We landed on a small airline just outside Quebec City. It was a small airport, the sort that might have once been used for flight training. I didn't know how the pavement was still in such good condition when the rest of the surrounding buildings looked utterly abandoned.

"Is this where we will be staying?" I asked as we landed. Distracted by puzzles or not, I was much happier to be solidly on the ground.

Josh shouldered a worn leather bag, "Just tonight. It's too far away from Chateau Frontenac or the rest of the city to be a proper home base while we're here." He ducked through the doorway, and stepped down onto the tarmac, "Arthur's going to hide the plane in one of those hangers."

102

"Will he be coming with us then?" I asked, knowing that Arthur wasn't officially on the team.

"Don't worry about Arthur," Arthur replied, stepping down from the plane last. "I'll be waiting here with the plane."

Merlin jabbed me in the ribs and handed me my bag, "Arthur likes to read. Every time he takes us anywhere, he gets through a small stack. Honestly, I don't know where he finds them all."

"That mansion has more in it than just dusty furniture and generators boy."

Merlin shrugged a bit and pulled on his backpack, "I suppose. Mm... so where to Josh?"

Josh nodded to the decrepit buildings just off from the tarmac, "Let's get settled away first. Then we'll make a trip into the city," he glanced up at the sun, not quite directly over us. "Late morning. We'll have plenty of time to explore the Chateau."

There was a fair amount of debris in the hanger that needed to be moved aside to fit the plane. Just after high noon, we were able to stop for lunch, and then gathered up whatever supplies we were going to need for a day trip into the city. We took enough food for our supper, water, flashlights, weapons, and a map. After promising Arthur that we would be returning that evening, we set out.

Due to the intensive study we had done of the area, we knew where the nearest bus stop was. From the airport, it was about an hour walk under the warm spring sun. I shed my jacket, holding it over my bad arm for this small part of the journey.

Once we were walking down the streets of houses, the first bus stop was at the end of the first block. It wasn't long before we heard the soft smooth hum of the essence engines pulling up to the curb.

Quebec City was unlike anything I had ever seen before. The city centre was like something out of a time machine. It was an old city and many of the stone houses still stood. The marketplace was just outside a seventeenth-century church called Notre-Dame-des-Victoires. The stalls spiralled around the square and up the twisting cobbled streets. There was an element of pride there. The buildings, old as they were, were well cared for. Spring flowers were planted in window boxes and the fleur-de-lis flew from every window and doorway. It was almost as if the riots never touched this part of the city.

In the square outside the church, there was a bust of a man on top of a stone pillar. The name Louis XIV was engraved near the bottom of the pillar.

"They called him the Sun King," Merlin whispered in my ear as we walked past. "I read that he sponsored eight hundred ladies to come here from France. He gave them all dowries and everything, hoping to get men here to settle down. They were called the Filles Du Roi or the King's Daughters."

"And here I thought you didn't like to read," I whispered back, nudging him in the ribs.

"It was in a history book about Quebec and I like history," Merlin corrected. "Arthur can keep all the classic fiction to himself."

Josh did like us knowing the history of a place but Merlin liked to dig a little deeper than necessary. Still, it was interesting. "So did all the King's Daughters get to live in the Chateau then?" I giggled, imagining stories of princesses in sweeping dresses and men in tailed coats dancing at a ball like in Pride and Prejudice.

"Err... no," Merlin looked up in the general direction of where the Chateau would be if we could see around buildings. "The Chateau was built as a hotel long after the King's daughters got here. It continued to be a hotel until the riots."

His hand slipped into mine. I liked that about Merlin, affection without the labels. When I first joined the resistance, it was too painful to think about what we were exactly. Grey had kissed me the night he died. Was I disrespecting his memory by being close with Merlin? In all these months, I had finally come to terms with my final memories of Grey. He was my closest friend, my brother in all but blood. Merlin and I were... something else. Merlin and I had been growing closer at a snail's pace, and I was perfectly content with that. I smiled up at him, hoping that before we left Quebec we might get some time to explore, maybe just the two of us.

The sprawling promenade suddenly opened up into a green space that hadn't been tended in years. It must have been lovely once upon a time. Overgrown trees shaded brushes and waist high grass. Just beyond that, was the Chateau.

It could have been a palace. I would have believed it if someone told me it was the King of France's vacation home. The stone building towered in all its crumbling glory, the carved facades weathered from years of being forgotten. Every floor used a different style of window. The entire left wing was a broken mass of stone. We had learned before we came, that the building was considered unsafe by New Atlantis and too costly to repair. Only the desperate would even think of going inside. I could see the allure, what with so many rooms hiding would be easy. Even with the left side little more than a crumbled mass of stone, the right side and the central tower looked solid enough.

"Alright everyone," Josh gathered us in a little group. "The rumours suggest it's a group in there. As you well know, they are likely frightened, and if they haven't discovered our treatment on their own then we need to assume that they think they are dying and have nothing to lose. Understood? Let's go."

Preferring to limit the number of people who saw us entering the building, we took a wide path around to the back. There were plenty of windows and doors at our level. Many of them were already broken. It was just a matter of picking one, and going inside.

The broken door we used led into what was once a dining room. Light spilt over the thousands of shards of broken glass. Josh took the lead, "We'll search the central tower first, floor by floor. Tasha, with me, we'll take the lead. Kalle and Braxton, guard the rear. The rest of you will be breaching rooms. Simon, Edgar, you will be entering the rooms first. If we're breaching two rooms at once, I want one of you in each group. Understand?" Tasha, Braxton, Simon and Edgar were the only ones trained with proper weapons. Therefore, they were the only ones handling guns. The rest of us had only our elements, which were not always the best in terms of precision.

A murmur of agreement swept over us and we shifted into a diamond-shaped formation. I was the least trained out of everyone else, but I felt ready for this. Goodness knew that we practised enough at the base. Floor by floor we twisted our way up the central tower of Chateau Frontenac. At all times, Josh and Tasha pushed forwards, while Kalle and Braxton made sure nothing snuck up behind us. With each door we passed, we breached the room in a circling rhythm. Every room was checked; every closet, bathroom, and ballroom.

I could see Josh was losing hope of us finding anyone here. Room after room was some version of the same beds, the same curtains, the same broken windows and looted rooms. The rich fabrics that might have once been stripes of yellow and dusty green were gnawed by rats and moths. Everything was coated with a thin layer of dust. Only our tracks showed any sign of activity for months.

It wasn't until the very top that we spotted something. We were in what must have been one of the nicest suites in the hotel. Josh pointed at tracks of dust that were not made by us. He and Tasha eased forward, following the tracks from the sitting room, to the master bedroom. More signs of habitation were strewn about the room: clothes, food, supplies, even toys. Things were left tipped over as if someone had tried to take them in a mad dash for escape. But where were they? The tracks didn't go out into the hall.

We searched the rest of the suite to no avail. At last, Josh sighed, "Hello? Bonjour? Nous sommes amis." We are friends. It was better than nothing.

"It's okay Josh. We still have that other wing to check," Kalle encouraged.

"And at least now we know that someone has been here recently," Elleen added.

Josh nodded, "Right, get back in formation. We'll head back down." Our entire group swung around, getting in the same diamond shape we had used on the way up. Josh started forward but stopped while we were still in the sitting area of the suite. He reached into his bag and pulled out a bit of food, leaving it on the couch. "If anyone is listening, it's just dried strawberries. We'll be back tomorrow around the same time. We would love if you came out to chat," uncertain if his message was heard or not, we began our descent to finish our search.

We didn't find any other signs of life. In a last attempt to appear friendly, we stopped to eat our supper in one of the downstairs ballrooms. No one came though at one point I swore I could hear someone walking nearby. Frank, who had a deep fear of ghosts, wanted to leave at once.

"Well, I guess we'll just go then," Josh said a little louder than necessary. Again he left a little food behind. "We'll be back again tomorrow," he repeated just a little louder and then we left.

Among the setting sun, we hurried to catch a bus back to the suburbs nearest the airport. The sky was a deep indigo with just a thin line of pink on the far horizon by the time made it all the way back.

Arthur was waiting for us, "I was starting to think you weren't coming back tonight," he said as we settled around the plane. I was so tired I could have fallen asleep there and then. I wrapped my sleeping blankets around me as I sat up and rubbed the ache from my calves.

"Did you find anyone at the Chateau?" Arthur put a pot of water on a small wood burning camp stove. He added herbs to the water making some kind of tea.

"Signs. Just signs. There are defiantly people there," Josh stood by the stove, watching the water come to a simmer. "I left some food. Hopefully, that'll be enough for one of them to at least come out tomorrow and say hi."

"So you still think there is more than one?" Merlin asked, and plopped down next to me

"That is my guess." Josh looked back at Merlin, "The number of supplies that were left in that room suggests, at least, a small group. That and few adults would bother keeping children's toys unless there were children with them."

Soon after, Arthur passed around cups of tea. It was pungent and earthy with a faint fruity sweetness. It warmed my insides and I settled down comfortably within my wrappings. Merlin laid down facing me.

"What did you think of your first day?" He whispered in the dark.

"Mmm...tried." I pulled the blankets up a little more. "Do you really think the people will come out to talk to us?"

Merlin kissed my forehead, "I think so. They're probably just waiting to see if we're New Atlantis or not."

"I hope so."

#

We rose with the sun the next morning. Arthur made us more tea to fight off the morning chill while eggs were cooked in a skillet and bread was passed around. I stayed wrapped in my blankets as I had my breakfast.

After eating we packed enough belongings for a couple days and stored the rest away in the plane. Arthur was already settled inside the plane, lounging in one of the leather seats with the rest of the tea and 'The Hound of the Baskervilles'. Promising to be back in a day or two, we set out for the city once again.

We didn't walk through the market this time, not wanting to catch too much attention with the amount of supplies we were carrying. Once again we took the wide path around to the back of the chateau and went through the broken door into the dining room. We hid our packs behind the old serving desk.

Everything was the same as before. Dusty corridors were illuminated by the light outside. First, we went to the ballroom where we had our supper the night before. Much to everyone's delight, the food Josh left behind was gone. We made the same sweeping search all the way up the central tower without running into a single person until at last, we found ourselves in the top floor suite we had left more food. Again, it was gone. We stepped into the main bedroom and found all the supplies had been taken away as well. I immediately looked over at Josh to see the light of hope draining from his face.

"Do you think they left?" I asked, looking for any sign that they might still be here somewhere.

"Perhaps..." Josh admitted, "If they didn't believe that we were friendly. Or if they believe us to be New Atlantis spies." He sighed and ran a hand through his hair, "It's a common problem and for good reason. New Atlantis has been known to send officers incognito into buildings like this."

"If you are New Atlantis spies, you would not be the first to try and find us," A voice spoke up from the sitting room. We scrambled around, facing an elderly woman standing in the middle of the room. "But the way you speak of the devils gives me some hope."

Josh motioned for everyone to keep their weapons down. He held his hands up in peace, "We are not New Atlantis. We are part of a resistance group working against them." He looked to me, "Would you mind showing your arm?"

I stepped forward and pulled up the sleeve of my jacket to reveal the tracery of quartz lines ingrained in my flesh. I had one of the easier to reveal marks. Merlin's mark was on his chest, Josh's on his back, Kalle's was on one of his legs, Frank's was hidden by his hair, and Elleen's was on her neck, covered in strategically placed makeup.

Seeing the mark on my arm had the expected effect, the woman recoiled and sucked in a breath. "All of you?"

Josh shook his head, "Six of us," he gestured to those of us with the illness. "The rest are sympathetic. You can trust them."

The woman pursed her lips, "Many of the uncured still believe the lies. Why should I trust them?"

Braxton, one of our completely healthy people, took a small step forward. "Ma'am. My mother was cured. I saw the change it created in her. When my little brother became sick, she was rough and unfeeling. He was scared and she wouldn't comfort him."

"Where are your brother and mother now?"

109

Braxton stood a little taller, "I imagine my mother is still in Ohio. My little brother is at the base of the resistance. He is well cared for and never received the cure."

The woman nodded, "You do not worry that it is a terminal illness?" The woman raised an eyebrow slightly,

"No Ma'am. There are other ways to slow the symptoms." Braxton replied.

The woman seemed satisfied by that answer. She did not question what Braxton said about another treatment. Instead, she looked to another one of the healthy ones. "You girl. What is your story?"

Tasha hesitated. Elleen gave her a little pat of encouragement, "I used to work as a nurse in the healing centres. I... I saw them when they came out of the pods..."

I couldn't help but shudder. I don't think I was the only one either.

That seemed to be enough for the woman to at least offer a little trust. She gestured to the door, "Let us go back down to that lovely ballroom where you had supper last night. Thank you for your gifts by the way. The children devoured the strawberries."

She led us back downstairs. As an act of good faith, Josh had everyone put their weapons away. We still had ample protection with our powers in any case.

When we reached the ballroom, it was still empty. The woman moved over to one of the walls and knocked on a particular section of bricks next to a faded painting. The solid brick wall folded open like curtains, letting at least a dozen people enter the room. They were all different ages. From the old man who opened the wall, to small children clutching at the legs of the adults.

"Come sit with us, share our food. I think we should compare notes on treatment."

CHAPTER NINE

Fieldwork

Her name was Marjorie. She and her husband Martin were originally from Montreal. Martin was the first to catch Telluria of the two of them, long before New Atlantis' cure. He discovered the powers by accident while moving rocks in his and Marjorie's garden. The food was scarce and if the disease took a nasty turn, he wanted to leave something that would support Marjorie. But in the process of moving rocks to expand the garden, the rocks began to move themselves.

She caught the disease a year later. By then, Martin was well aquatinted with his powers and was able to help her with her fire. Even after the cure was discovered, neither bothered to get it. The disease wasn't affecting them like other people, and they thought others who needed the cure more should get it first.

The trouble started when their neighbours were cured. They knew that Marjorie and Martin were sick. New Atlantis was called, arguments were made, and a New Atlantis van was tipped over. The pair of them packed a bag and headed north, eventually arriving in Quebec City. Following a gut feeling, they decided to never get cured.

They heard the stories of the cured. They saw first hand how the cure changed fine lovely people into apathetic loyalists. No one was talking about the powers or how it stopped Telluria's spread. Martin and Marjorie made it their mission to tell as many of the sick as they could and to offer guidance to those who didn't want the cure.

They chose to hide in the Chateau Frontenac for several reasons. One, it was close enough to the marketplace that supplies were easy to come by. Two, the building was considered unfit, so no one ever came to visit. And three, if anyone did come to visit, Martin and the other stone elementals had such a maze of passages built between the walls that no one would ever find them unless they wanted to be found.

Marjorie told their story over a meal of flatbread and boiled eggs. After she was done, Josh told ours. He told them of Marcus and how he had worked for New Atlantis on the cure. He told them how Marcus had seen just how wrong it was and knew there was another way. Josh told them all about the base, how it was well hidden, protected, and everyone was cared for.

"We would love it if you would consider coming back with us," Josh assured them. We were sitting in a loose circle in the middle of the ballroom. Marjorie's group was on one side, us on the other. "However, if you would rather stay, we offer our support. There's a network of resistance chapters around the globe. We have connections with most of them though few prefer to remain independent."

Marjorie looked to her husband, much was said in the space of their silence. "We will have to consider your offer." She gestured to the children. There was nearly one child for every adult. Their needs and safety would always be considered first. "How long will you be visiting the city?"

"We are prepared for a week. Though our Terra has a talent for finding food in the wild, we may be able to stretch it until two." Josh lifted his hand to his heart in a motion of sincerity, "Our primary aim was to contact you and offer whatever support you believe is best. Though I must say you are doing very well on your own."

"It is only food we are short of." Marjorie wrung her hands. After the long winter, even the children's faces were slightly more angular than one might expect. "We often have resorted to stealing from the ration warehouse. We've almost been caught too many times to count. The only trouble with being so far in the city is there is no place to have a garden. Certainly not without attracting attention. Martin and Leeroy can fish. Power is a minor need, and the water still works in many of the rooms."

Josh nodded, as if weighing their problems in his mind, "Our base is completely self-sufficient." He began, much to the awe of some of the Quebec adults. "But there are other ways. A resistance chapter in Berlin fakes ration accounts. It may work for you as well. You only need a home where it can be delivered."

As Josh, Marjorie and Martin continued to discuss possibilities, I noticed the half dozen or so children, all under age 10, were getting restless. Curious about the strangers in their midst and excited for new people to play with, the children approached us. Braxton and Simon were pulled into a game of catch with two young boys. A little girl had taken a shine to Kalle's shoulder length blonde hair; he was letting her braid it.

A hand slipped into mine. Beside me Merlin's face was bright, his grey eyes were like the sun through the clouds. "Pity cameras aren't a thing anymore. I would love to get a picture of Kalle right now."

"Don't be mean." I chastised playfully, "It's... um... very chivalrous of him." Though in saying that I had to smother a giggle.

Merlin gave my hand a little squeeze, "I could ask her to do your hair next." He appraised my hair, which I imagined was a frizzy mess.

In retaliation, I punched him lightly in the ribs, "Don't you dare. I know where you sleep."

"For the next week, beside you." His grin spread as his chest puffed out just a little, "Which, I must say is much better than listening to Cyrus snoring."

Warmth flooded my cheeks and I dropped my gaze to watch Braxton and Simon again, "Cyrus doesn't snore... too loudly."

"How would you know?" Merlin asked, and I could hear his mind whirling trying to think of a time I would have heard Cyrus snoring.

I looked back up at him, "Oh that better not be jealousy I hear." I giggled, deciding not to prolong his agony. "I live with Ember remember. She told me that their rooms used to be next to each other in their old house. According to her, he only sounded like a miniature sputtering chainsaw."

"A miniature sputtering chainsaw?" Merlin sounded incredulous, enough that Frank looked over at us curiously, "Maybe a chainsaw with a cold. At least, I don't snore."

I thought back to the night before, the soft sound of Merlin's breathing next to me. "Oh yes, you do." I corrected him. "I heard it." He did technically snore, but so light and soft that it was more akin to a purr.

Merlin was flabbergasted. "I... but... no. You're just making that up!"

I bat my eyelashes at him, "Would I really do a thing like that? It's true."

Merlin was left with his mouth agape as Josh came over to us. He waved for everyone to gather round, "We're staying here tonight." He said in a soft voice. "Marjorie And Martin have agreed that we may stay here in the ballroom."

"Do they sleep here too?" Tasha asked.

Josh shook his head, "They have their own place hidden in the Chateau. Marjorie wouldn't tell me where, though I suspect that Martin may have built something within the rubble on the ruined side. Even we didn't think of looking there, simply because we overlooked the possibility of them already discovering their powers."

I frowned, remembering the supplies we found in the central tower. "What about upstairs?"

A strange little smile pulled at Josh's lips. "The kids get bored being cooped up all the time. They make a bit of an adventure out of staying in the other suites from time to time."

I shuddered at the idea of never being able to go outside. As a kid, I spent most of my time outdoors, perhaps mostly because of my Father. Also, because outside was the only place I could be truly useful to my parents. I could gather food, tend the garden, or just be out of their way as they went about their work.

"So, we found people here. Rather quickly I might add." Kalle ran his fingers through his hair, undoing all the little braids the little girl had put in. "What's the plan now?"

"Our main focus is still this group," Josh reminded us. "We need to earn their trust and help them as best we can. They are doing quite well for themselves, but they could use some help. Food in particular." Josh pulled his bag off his back and took out a pen and paper. He scrawled a long message and handed it to Simon and Edgar, "I want to two of you to bring this to Marcus. Arthur will take you. Unless Marcus says otherwise, come back as soon as you can."

Josh then looked to Merlin, Kalle, Frank, and me. "I want you four to go out in the city, try to find anyone who's hiding a mark, anyone who might be sympathetic. You know what to do."

"What about you Josh?" Merlin asked, already reaching for his jacket.

"Elleen, Tasha, Braxton, and I are going to stay here. We'll try to make friends hm?"

#

And so the team split up. Simon and Edgar left to catch the next bus back to the airport. Josh, Elleen, Tasha and Braxton stayed in the Chateau, offering help where they could and listening to the needs of the group. The rest of us walked out into the Quebec spring air to spend our days walking the streets.

It was a rather pleasant task admittedly. On that first day, the clouds covered the high spring sun. The air was still balmy and a soft breeze caressed our faces. We walked around the marketplace and branched out further into the historic city. Notre-Dame-des-Victoires was apparently not the only Notre Dame in Quebec City. There was another one, larger, grander, and older some ways down the road. It was strange to see the ruins of buildings barely twenty years old next to the untouched historic sites that have been standing for hundreds. It said something about the craftsmanship of times gone past when stone was the mark of a sturdy house, not wood and gypsum.

115

Day by day, we didn't spot anyone. It did not surprise us. If someone was out there, they were doing all they could to not be noticed. Even so, the time was not completely wasted. We took to walking past the market every evening, trading things we had found around the city for new supplies and toys to bring back to the Chateau.

I made a point of filling Merlin's backpack with as much food as could be found; wild garlic and dandelions mostly. I got lucky one day and found a patch of fiddleheads in a park. That night we fried them with garlic and the fish Martin and Leeroy caught.

Simon and Edgar returned after two days with more food, plenty enough to share with those at the Chateau. Marcus must have been trying to make a good impression as he included a small bag of precious coffee beans and a tin of candied nuts as a gift. There were all the things you couldn't find in the wild; flour, sugar, salt, and a full sack of cornmeal. There was also bottles of jam and dried fruit from the summer past.

One of the men knew how to make cornbread and we had the sweet yellow cakes for dessert with the fish and fiddleheads.

The week sped on. In a way, it went too fast. We never found anyone else who might be hiding the mark. It wasn't easy to find someone hiding from the common enemy. It was decided that Marjorie, Martin and the others would try to stay in Quebec. It was their home after all and they could be here to help others. It would be easier in the summer when food was plentiful if you knew where to look. They would discuss it again next fall when they would know how prepared they were for another winter. Two of the other adults volunteered to come back with us for a time, to learn all they could and bring back the knowledge. Plans for acquiring electricity were being made. Martin and one of the other women, an earth elementalist like himself, were making plans to expand their living quarters in the ruined side of the Chateau to move beneath the ground.

On the last day, Merlin and I were strolling hand in hand on the sunlit sprawling cobbled streets of the marketplace. It was nearly high noon, and Josh would be expecting us. Frank and Kalle were just behind us, perusing the stalls and haggling with the locals in mixed English and

French. Of all of us, Kalle had the best grasp of the language. I could hear him over the crowd, trilling off the deep rolling rhythm of the words. I only understood one word in ten, but it was nice to listen to.

"I like it here, but it'll be nice to be going back." I murmured softly. I missed Ember and Cyrus. I missed the day to day patterns of the base. The nice thing about adventures was eventually going home.

Merlin picked a flower out of one of the window boxes. It was a white lily with lines of yellow and orange running along the petals. He threaded the stem over my ear. The sunlight was shining in his eyes, it made me imagine the sun shining through storm clouds. "I don't know. I think the French air suits you." He touched my cheek, brushing his thumb against my jaw. "Beats florescent lights and being underground all the time anyway."

I could feel the blood warning my cheeks though I couldn't exactly tell why. "Just cause we're going back, doesn't mean we can't go outside."

Merlin breathed in the fresh spring air. "I was thinking... perhaps when we go back after we get settled in and Ember has finished interrogating us for all the details, maybe we could do something together. Maybe a picnic or..." He trailed off, letting the idea simply linger between us.

I stopped and looked up at him. He circled his arms around my waist as we stood in the ebb and flow of foot traffic. "Like a date?" I asked, tilting my head slightly.

Merlin rubbed the back of his neck. "Well... if you wanted." Red splotches were on his cheeks that I hadn't noticed before. Was he blushing? "I've been meaning to ask for ages. But... I thought you deserved some time for your thoughts. After what happened to your friend and all."

My heart swelled. I never considered before that he was holding back for my sake. I curled my hand around his neck and pulled him down to kiss me. His lips moved over mine. I could taste salt and strawberries. He smelled like the world after the rain. The sun shone on my closed eyes, illuminating my world into a sea of red-gold.

I would have happily stayed right there forever. Or in the very least to slowly linger, to take his hand at the last possible moment and make our way back to Chateau Frontenac and say our goodbyes.

"Merlin! Terra!"

A hand landed on my shoulder and the spell was broken. Blinking, I looked up at Frank. He was pale and his eyes were wide. "You need to see this. Like, now."

His expression was so jarring I couldn't help but feel the first waves of panic. I followed his gaze to the New Atlantis projection billboard. It was splashed across the surface of several small buildings. The image of a new van was rotating with a marquee of text beneath it. "The newest advancement in maintaining the health of our global community. Select patrolling vans will now be equipped with Telluria sensing radar. Infected citizens can be sensed within a quarter kilometre radius. We ask all citizens to cooperate with New Atlantis officers. If you hear the sirens, please remain calm. Infected citizens will be taken to the closest available healing facility. Remember that Telluria is highly contagious to those who have not previously contracted the disease. For the health of your families, your friends, and your community, we offer this technology as our continued fight against this horrible virus."

I could hear my pulse. My hands were numb. We looked at each other; Merlin, Frank, Kale and I. A long mute second held between us in absolute understanding. This would change everything.

We couldn't run without drawing attention to ourselves. We were on the far side of the market, a good couple kilometres from the Chateau at least. Merlin took my hand, squeezing as the four of us picked up pace. There was a choking press of people vying to read the notice. Members of the crowd were cheering. My stomach knotted in pity for the poor fools who believed this was a good idea.

Sirens filled out ears before we made it around the first turn. "They didn't waste time did they." Kalle bit a curse under his breath. "Better run. We don't know how accurate those things are."

We threw caution to the wind and ran.

"Please remain calm. Would the infected citizen please come with us. Everything will be okay." The clear soothing voice blasted from a loudspeaker mounted to the van. Too late we realized that running was a mistake. Around us, cruel, twisted faces were turning our way.

A gnarled hand grabbed my arm. "What's the rush? You're the one, aren't you?

Frank hauled the man off me. More hands were grabbing us. The crowd had become a hive with a single purpose. They pushed in around us, blocking our way. No one was trying to hurt us, only to hold us until the officers waded through the crowd.

"I think we're going to have to do something drastic," Merlin called out, struggling to wrestle off a pair who held his arms.

"Terra. A tunnel or something would be nice right about now." Suggested Frank, fairing only slightly better than Merlin.

I yelped as a hand yanked on my hair, "We would be running blind. There's no way to tell direction down there." Not to mention I didn't want to run into a sewer pipe. "We just need to get the people out of the way."

"On it!" Merlin stamped his foot. Water flowed between the stones of the cobbled street, it burst from nearby pipes, or pulled out of the sea-soaked air. It surrounded the four of us in a watery shell. The cured still held on, acting on what the compulsion told them to do, but I saw fear and awe enter many faces.

Merlin stamped his foot again. Like a tidal wave, the water burst out in all directions. The hoard immediately around us knocked back.

We broke into a run. Merlin kept the water swirling around us, pushing anyone out of the way. Kalle guarded the rear, making the ground shake and crumble in our wake. Anyone who missed Merlin's water was slipping on crumbling stones or stumbling over themselves.

We were still trapped by the twisting streets, however. I rose my hands and a bridge of stone lifted us from roof to roof. We ran until we lost the crowds below us, and we were out of range from the vans. All I could hear was water, stone and my thunderous heart.

The ringing had nearly faded from my ears when the siren started again. I built a bridge up the last leg before the Chateau, and we realized that this time we were running towards the sound.

"Oh God no." I breathed, praying that New Atlantis would find no one. That Martin would tunnel everyone out of range.

They had found someone. Josh must have come out to see if we were back yet. He alone was being dragged towards the van by two officers. He was physically struggling, not yet resorting to using his powers like we did.

"Hey Frank, I think the weather called for a hurricane." Merlin mused aloud, looking up at the sky. It was a beautiful day with whips of white clouds far in the distance. Despite that, it began to rain. A drizzle turned into buckets just in the small area where the officers were wrestling Josh into the van.

"I think you're right Merlin." Frank agreed. There was only a light breeze around us, but hurricane force winds buffeted the officers. Josh slipped from their grip and made a break for it. When they tried to pursue, despite their difficulties, they found themselves having to dodge stone walls that appeared out of nowhere.

This could not go on for long. The rain was already starting to fade as Merlin was coming to the end of his strength. The officers weren't relenting, driven by the compulsion of the cure. I took a breath and raised my hands. Pillars of stone burst through the ground around the officers. Crossbars formed, effectively caging them in.

The storm faded and Josh jogged over to the van. After a moment of tinkering, the sirens shut off. "Thank you," He said as we caught up. "I'm not sure I would have been able to take them myself."

He was flushed and soaked to the skin, but otherwise unharmed. "Kalle, Frank, could you go tell the others to gather their things. It is time to go."

"Everyone?" Frank asked, raising an eyebrow slightly.

Josh nodded, reading the question in Frank's eyes, "Everyone." He then glanced at the officers, who were trying to chisel their way out of their cage like a pair of rabid dogs. "Do tell Nikolai that Marcus sends his regards."

The three of us waited outside, keeping guard over the officers. We didn't want to hurt them if it wasn't necessary, they didn't know better after all. Thankfully, Frank and Kalle didn't take long. Everyone, including Marjorie's and Martin's group, was coming out of a hole Martin made in the wall of the Chateau.

"What happened?" Martin asked, closing the wall once everyone was out. He glanced at the caged officers cautiously.

"It's not safe here for you anymore." Josh began to explain, an apologetic tone in his voice, "We know another place. Everything will be explained on the way." It was better not to talk in front of the officers. "Unfortunately, we'll need to borrow their van. I think we can all squeeze in. Would you be willing to get rid of it after we've left Martin?"

Martin nodded and turned back to his group. By his direction, everyone began piling into the back of the van, children held in the laps of their parents.

"You too," Josh said to Merlin and I. We were still lingering around the officers, waiting for everyone else to be ready. Kalle was climbing into the driver's seat.

Feeling slightly numb, I nodded and turned with Merlin to climb into the van. We should have been more careful. After the fight to get to the Chateau, we must have fancied ourselves invincible. We never considered the idea that the officers might still have weapons until we heard a click and a crack that broke the air.

My ears were still ringing when Merlin touched his own torso with a curiously blank expression. It wasn't until his fingers came away wet with blood that either of us realized what happened.

Merlin stumbled forward and I caught his arm. Blood was staining his blue t-shirt. "Merlin. Merlin." My voice didn't sound like my own. It was too high, too fast. Other hands pulled him into the van. I jumped in behind him, and the doors slammed shut. I was pulling off my jacket and pressing it against his wound before I properly knew what I

121

was doing. "Merlin you stay with me. Don't you dare leave me." I whispered, my voice only just starting to break under the strain.

The van's tires squealed and Merlin groaned as the van lurched into motion. "Wouldn't dream of it." He murmured with half-lidded eyes. He reached for my hand, his fingers pale and cold against mine.

My eyes flicked up to his. A thousand different nightmares flitting through my mind.

"It won't happen again," he whispered, reading something on my face. With that promise, his body slumped and he closed his eyes.

My heart stopped. "Merlin! Merlin wake up!" I wanted to shake him but couldn't risk letting go of the wound. As far as I could tell, the bullet was still in there somewhere.

"Keep pressure, Terra." Josh put two fingers against Merlin's neck. "His heart is still strong. Just keep pressure. We can treat it on the plane." There was no room there, with the three of us squeezed into the back corner of the van. Thankfully the road was smooth, Kalle or Martin was probably making it that way.

Arthur was waiting for us at the airport. The plane was pulled out of the hanger and sitting ready on the tarmac. "What happened?" He demanded, not expecting the stolen van or so many people.

Josh hopped out the back and put a hand on Arthur's shoulder, "There's been an accident. We need to leave now."

Arthur all but ran back to the plane. Josh stepped aside with Martin and Marjorie to explain that they could hide in the airport for as long as they liked. I didn't hear all that was being said. I was walking with Kalle and Frank, keeping the pressure on Merlin's bullet wound as they carried him on the plane. I looked back just long enough to see Marjorie wave goodbye.

CHAPTER TEN

Healing

The flight lasted an eternity. In that time, Elleen and Josh, our best healers, peeled Merlin out of his shirt and treated the wound to the best of their ability. Josh was encouraged that the bleeding had stopped and Merlin's heartbeat kept a strong steady rhythm. There was still the worry that the bullet was left inside. I couldn't entertain the idea of it moving. I focused only on that he was still alive in that moment.

Merlin didn't wake. I sat on the floor next to him, his hand clasped in my own. Even as we landed and people from the med bay came swarming in, I didn't let go. Not until he was loaded onto a stretcher and the medical staff were lifting him away did Josh pull me back from following. Merlin's hand slipped from mine as he was carried away.

"He's in good hands, Terra," Josh said softly, a comforting hand on my shoulder.

He led me out of the plane. I felt unsteady. There was a buzzing between my eyes and the world seemed fuzzy, "What if..." My mouth closed over the words unable to finish.

"They are going to get the bullet out. He'll be in surgery for a while, it's delicate work. But listen to me Terra," We stopped and Josh put both hands on my shoulders, "Merlin is strong, and a water type. I believe he can pull through. Do you?"

I bobbed my head in a small nod. Water types were known for healing faster than most. "When can I see him?"

123

"It's going to take some time. Why don't you go to your room, unpack your things, maybe find your friends and tell them what's going on." Josh smiled weakly and handed me my bag, "The waiting will be easier if you're distracted."

I didn't know how to not think about Merlin, but I nodded and went inside. I ran into blissfully few people as I took the long way back to my room. It was late afternoon and Ember wasn't there. I guessed she was either still in the workshop or at supper. My stomach gave an uncomfortable lurch at the idea of food. I would probably skip that as a possible distraction. Instead, I methodically took all of my belongings out of my bag and laid them on the bed. I sorted and put everything away. After this activity I glanced at the clock hopefully, barely fifteen minutes had passed.

I was still covered in blood, so I stripped off my clothes and kicked them aside before getting in the shower. I stood under the water and let it simply run over me. Least in there, I couldn't feel the buzzing anymore. The water felt like rain and my heart clenched painfully. It was strange. When Grey died I was in hysterics. I curled up in a cave and cried my eyes out for hours. But with Merlin, I was just numb. Everything felt as though it was taking place apart from myself. I didn't know if this was a calm before the crash, but at least I could function.

I dressed in clean clothes and left. If I wasn't going to go have supper the only thing left to do was wait. There didn't seem much difference in waiting in my room or waiting in the med bay. There wasn't a waiting room per se but there were some chairs in the hall outside the doors to the surgery. I sat down, folded my hands in my lap and simply waited.

It was another half hour before I heard footsteps. Glancing down the hall, a shock of red hair entered my line of sight. "Terra!" Ember rushed to me and pulled me into a hug. "Are you okay?! I went to our room to clean up for supper and I saw the blood and-"

My hands remained in my lap. Cyrus was there too, hands in his pockets and standing a few feet away, "Not my blood." I didn't recognize my own voice. It was too throaty, too soft.

"Not..." Ember pulled away. I studied her face as the realization came to burn there, "Where's Merlin?! Terra, he's not-"

I shook my head, stopping her mid-sentence. I didn't want the numbness to shatter just yet, "H-he got shot. In the stomach. His heartbeat was strong when they took him in."

"How long ago was that?" Cyrus stepped forward, his question cutting in before Ember had fully processed what I said.

"It happened around noon." I sounded like I was talking about something as mundane as a rainstorm. Or a hurricane. I checked the time, "He's been in surgery for a little over an hour."

"Oh... Oh God." Ember's hands flew to her mouth, "How..."

I sighed wishing that I didn't have to repeat the story so soon. But if I were going to crash it was probably better with Ember and Cyrus there. They've been there for me when I was at my worst before. I started my story in the marketplace from the moment we saw the announcement on the projection screen. I explained the sensors and how we had set one off moments after hearing about them. I told them how we had had to use our powers in front of the entire marketplace to escape only to find that New Atlantis were waiting at the Chateau as well. My throat tightened as I told them about the fight, the cage, and at last the gunshot. I kept my hands clasped tightly in my lap to hide the shaking, "We were stupid. We should have searched the officers. In the very least I should have made the walls solid." I closed my eyes, willing the sound of gunshots to go away, "God... you should have seen his face..."

"Terra." Cyrus knelt in front of me, gently loosening the grip between my hands. When I looked at him, his image was distorted. I realized I crying. "You don't need to say anymore. It's okay."

"It most certainly is not okay!" Ember was pacing the small width of the hallway, hands gesticulating as she talked, "They shot him! For no other reason than that stupid compulsion."

I wiped my eyes with the back of my sleeve. The hall was getting warmer than usual.

125

"Em sit down." Cyrus chastised his little sister, "You can burn something later."

"Cy what if they killed him! It's not as bad as being cured no but-" She turned on Cyrus, "He's your best friend for crying out loud! Can't you be just a little more worried?"

I really didn't want to listen to Cyrus and Ember fight. I didn't want to listen to the possibility of Merlin's death. I leaned forward in my chair and covered my ears. Ember remained in my line of sight though everything she said now sounded muffled. Cyrus rubbed my back. I didn't hear the deeper rumble of his voice, he must have been letting Ember go on her tirade.

My reaction I realized wasn't a result of not being able to handle Merlin getting hurt. I took the position in the recruitment team knowing that it would be dangerous. It was the way it happened; the kiss, the warning, the shot. There were too many parallels with what happened to Grey. It was too soon and it felt like a wound being reopened.

After a while, Cyrus tapped on my arm. I lifted my head to the surgeon who had come out to talk to us. "Merlin is out of surgery." She began, there were spots of blood on her scrubs.

Ember hugged herself, "How is he? Can we see him?"

The doctor shook her head, "Not yet. He's in recovery at the moment." She paused, looking between the three of us, "We were able to extract the bullet. There was minimal internal damage. He was very lucky."

"But will he be okay?" Ember repeated and I was glad that she was asking the questions I so wanted to hear.

"I believe so yes." But before we could feel truly relieved, the doctor put up her hands in caution, "There is always a chance of infection or internal bleeding but as of right now he is doing well."

"Theresa, can't we see him? Just for ease of mind? It would only be a moment." Cyrus implored, "Please?"

Theresa hesitated but shook her head, "We will move him as soon. I'm afraid you can't see him until then. I'm sorry Cyrus, it is simply protocol."

Cyrus slumped with a small sigh, "I understand,"

With a small nod, Theresa walked back into the surgery. Cyrus turned to me, "He's going to be okay Terra. Merlin is a stubborn goat and he would never let something like an infection take him out. He's going to be fine."

"But what if-"

Cyrus placed his hand on my back again, "You can't live in what if's. You'll go mad."

I conceding, seeing the pointlessness in that train of thought. I sat back in the chair and hugged my arms around myself.

Cyrus stood, "I'm going to get us something to drink. I'll be right back, okay?" He looked at me when he asked this.

I nodded and Cyrus soon disappeared down the hall. Ember sat down next to me, and I leaned over and put my head on her shoulder. She was warm like someone running a fever. "Do you really think he'll be okay?" I croaked out the question, "Cyrus seems confident."

Ember was sitting up straight, her body was tight, "I'm sure he'll be fine." She grit out between clenched teeth.

"Ember... what's the matter?" If she really believed Merlin would be fine, I didn't understand why she was so wound up. Even for Ember, this was a bit much.

"Nikolai is what's the matter."

There was that name again. "Who is he?" I coughed to clear my strained voice, "Josh mentioned him. He told the officers to tell Nikolai that Marcus sends his regards."

A harsh laugh grated past Ember's teeth, "Nikolai Wolfe is the head of New Atlantis. You don't hear about him much simply because he wants New Atlantis to appear as a community rather than a dictatorship."

"Did you ever meet him?" I knew that Marcus had been far up in New Atlantis. Maybe Ember got to meet this Nikolai guy at the company Christmas party or something like that.

"Yeah... we knew him." Ember's tone had softened, with just an edge of bitterness, "He and Father were good friends once. Nikolai was like an uncle to me and Cy. They thought they could change the world..." Ember sat back in her chair. I moved my head off her shoulder, "They had a falling out after Mother died. She was fire too, like me. The cure was still in the early stages then, they couldn't save her."

My heart ached for my own parents. I knew that Ember and Cyrus's mother was gone, but neither talked about it. "I'm sorry," It was a lame form of condolences, but it was all I had at the moment.

Ember waved a hand, "It's alright. It was a long time ago." And yet and I could still hear the hurt in her voice.

I bit my lip, morbid curiosity pulling at me, "What was the falling out about?"

Ember frowned slightly, "Father said it was over the cure. He didn't agree with Nikolai that it was the only way. They knew about the powers but Nikolai refused to use them. He called the whole thing an abomination."

Cyrus returned with three steaming mugs of tea. "I caught Arthur in the kitchen making tea. He was glad to share."

I looked down at the steaming mug. Rose hips and dried strawberries were floating in the pink stained water. "Thanks," I said softly, taking a sip. Arthur must have added a little honey as well.

The three of us sipped our tea in relative silence. Occasionally I found myself pulling on the jade pendant at my throat. If I could, I would have willed my powers to heal him. Too bad earth didn't have that sort of talent, none of the elements did.

It was another hour before the doors to the surgery opened and Merlin was wheeled out on a gurney. His skin was ghostly pale with only a flush of colour on his cheeks. One of the med staff walked behind him holding the IV line high.

In unison, Cyrus, Ember, and I got up and followed to Merlin's recovery room. We stood back as Merlin was wheeled over to a small brass bed. With some of the most careful air powers I ever saw, he was lifted onto the bed. He gave a little groan from the movement but his eyes remained closed. After a quick check to make sure everything was fine the healing staff left us with him.

There were dark circles under Merlin's eyes. The muscles in his face shifted cracking a half smile, "Cy?"

"Yeah?"

"On a scale from one to ten, how badly did Ember freak out?"

Cyrus tilted his head to and fro, "For Em... a 4. No scorch marks and the temperature didn't get above 30."

Merlin chuckled and winced as the moment upset his wound.

Ember and I must have looked absolutely incredulous. After a half-second thought, I marched up and punched Merlin in the arm.

"Ow Terra! It's not nice to punch a dog when he's down you know." Merlin reached up and weakly rubbed his arm, eyeing my clenched fist like I might punch him again.

"You had me worried senseless you idiot!" The hours of waiting with my stone heart were finally shattering around me, "I thought you were going to die! I was sitting there, seeing your stupid face in my head telling me it wouldn't happen again." I made air quote for emphasis. Merlin's face was satisfyingly stunned, "And the first bloody words out of your mouth are asking if Ember had a hissy fit!"

Merlin was fully awake now. He looked wounded, his brows furrowing, "Terra I-"

I crossed my arms, ignoring the hot tears threatening to fall. "Yes?"

Merlin opened and closed his mouth, eventually deciding on what to say, "Were you really worried I would die?"

I was reaching the end of my wits. I brushed away the first tears starting to fall, "Yes you fool. Last time someone I cared about got shot, it didn't end well. Remember?"

A flicker of emotion went across Merlin's face. His expression softened and he reached out his hand, "Come here."

I made the single step forward and dropped my arms. My hand slipped into his, my anger dwindling like a smothered flame.

He gave my fingers a little squeeze, "I said it won't happen again because I knew you would think that way. I knew I wasn't going to die. I didn't want you to worry for nothing."

I looked down at our joined hands, "Well you passed out before you could explain that bit." I pointed out, my voice turning soft.

"I was a little preoccupied," a smile touched his lips, "Forgive me?"

I sighed, and wiped away the falling tears again, "I'm not mad at you."

The shine of humour lit his eyes, "Could have fooled me."

I let out a sigh, "I'm mad at myself. This is all my fault."

Ember blinked in confusion, "Why? You didn't shoot him." She pointed out.

I shook my head, "No but as good as. I wasn't thinking. I was the one who made the cage. I should have just made the walls solid." I closed my eyes. I didn't know what I would have done if there was another death on my head, "I'm sorry Merlin."

Merlin pulled lightly on my hand. I opened my eyes again, unable to stop the tears rolling down my cheeks, "It was a mistake anyone could have made. No one else thought of a gun. Kalle or Martin could have fixed the cage but they didn't."

I bit my lip. I had to admit that he was right but it didn't make me feel any better.

"Em. I think this is our cue to leave." Cyrus whispered, loud enough that I could hear him.

"But we just got here." She protested.

Cyrus went to the door, "Merlin needs rest." He offered a small smile at Merlin, "We'll come visit again tomorrow."

Sighing, Ember conceding and gave Merlin a quick peck on the cheek. "Get well soon. I want a turn at punching you as well."

"In that case, I'll stay injured as long as possible."

"Very funny." Ember murmured, and she and Cyrus left.

Merlin and I were left in a heavy silence. I sucked in a breath and wiped away the ebbing tears. Merlin tugged on my hand, "Will you lie down with me?" He asked, patting the side of the bed.

Mindful of his injury, I climbed onto the bed and settled beside him. "I thought I lost you." I repeated, my voice small and broken, "I didn't... I didn't know how to handle it. It was all happening again..." I laid my head down on his shoulder.

Merlin laced his fingers through my hair. Gently he twirled a lock around his finger, "I'm not going anywhere. Face it, Terra, you're stuck with me." Even without looking at him, I could hear the smile in his voice, but it soon faded, "You don't regret joining the recruitment team, do you? I can't promise it'll get easier. Worse seems more likely.

I raised my head and kissed him quickly to shut him up, "Not a chance. I want to help people. We'll just need to be more careful."

Merlin sighed heavily, "No more long walks in the city together I suppose."

"Not like you're walking for a while anyway." I pointed out, "I guess this means our date is postponed.

Merlin shifted in bed, arranging his face to look like I had personally offended his manhood, "I was shot in the stomach. Not the legs. Mark my words the moment I'm free of this bed we are going on that date."

I couldn't hold back the giggle. I leaned up and kissed the tip of his nose, "Well Josh will be glad that you'll be trapped here long enough to write your report."

Merlin gave a long exaggerated groan, "Oh I am far too injured for that. Couldn't you do it for me?"

"Certainly not!" I rested my head back on his shoulder, "We'll do it together."

I felt him kiss the top of my head, "Okay."

#

Merlin was held in the med bay for over a week. During that time I sat with him during the day, leaving only for meals. Ember and Cyrus came to visit each evening. Sometimes we played cards or something that Ember called element charades. A game where you make an object of your power for the others to guess. I pulled out a bit of sand to help Cyrus' creations be visible.

Nine days since his surgery, I walked into the med bay room to find Merlin dressed and out of bed. He was packing his few belongings. "What's going on?" I asked. We were told he would be staying two weeks at least.

Merlin took me in his arms and kissed me, "I'm free! I promised to be on my best behaviour and check in every day. They couldn't see why I couldn't go back to my own room."

I giggled with delight. The room was enough to make someone stir crazy. "You do know that Ember is going to fuss right?"

He turned and packed away the rest of his things in a duffle bag. "Maybe we can put off the inevitable and hide?" He said in such a way to suggest he was planning something.

I picked up his bag and hoisted it onto my shoulder, "Did you have something in mind?"

Merlin reached for my hand, "How about instead of the dining hall, you and I have a little picnic in the solarium?"

I raised an eyebrow slightly, "That sounds like a date."

Putting a finger under my chin, he lowered his face down to mine. I was surrounded by the smell of the air after a storm. He tasted like toothpaste and his lips moved achingly sweet over mine, "Maybe it is a date."

"Supper isn't for hours." I reminded him. It was in fact, just after breakfast.

"Oh." Merlin's mouth quirked into a tilted smile, "I think we can find something to do with the time."

The warmth was spreading through my cheeks. I looked up at him.

"I just want to be with you," Merlin added. He took my hand again, lacing his fingers through mine, "Anytime spent with you will be time well spent I think."

I tilted my head, a grin touching my lips, "We need to drop off your things first. Then we'll see."

"Sounds like a plan."

CHAPTER ELEVEN

Power

With Merlin still recovering, and no upcoming missions, things were slow. Even with daily physical training and Josh's insistence that we continue to study other languages and cultures, we still found ourselves with large empty chunks of time. The recruitment team had been effectively grounded until further notice. I took to volunteering in the greenhouse and gardens. With spring in full swing, the first crops were being planted. Turnips and cabbages were blooming out in the gardens while beds of potatoes and carrots were coming up in the greenhouse.

Weeks passed and there were still no missions for the recruitment team. Marcus was being cautious, sending out only those who wouldn't trip the New Atlantis sensors. Arthur was flying daily with Simon, Braxton, Tasha or Edgar, checking on the other bases in some vain hope that someone had found a solution for the sensors. While there was nothing on that front yet, there was news from Martin and Marjorie. They were flourishing in their new base. The children loved playing outside for the first time in years and Martin was expanding underground.

Other areas were not as lucky. A chapter in California was found by the sensors. Arthur and Braxton told us how the base, a previously abandoned apartment building, held all the signs of a raid. They had stayed for several days but never found survivors.

Not all was lost, however. Arthur and Braxton brought back the sensor from the New Atlantis van we left in Quebec. Marcus was certain that we would be able to find a way to jam the signal. The sooner the better. Messages from other chapters were trickling in asking for help.

We were left in limbo. Spring turned to summer. Merlin's wound healed and he re-joined the rest of us in physical training. There were no updates until mid-July when during lunch Marcus stood on his bench amid a sea of faces with a small nondescript box held over his head. "I am pleased to announce that after weeks of work, we have found a way to mask the Telluria signal."

The hall erupted into cheers. Marcus motioned for everyone to settle down so that he could finish, "This box emits a small signal that jams the sensors. It is strong enough to hide us while we're in a passive state. However," Marcus lowered the box, slipping it into his pocket. "The moment you use your powers, the sensors will be able to pick you up again. For those of you who have dealings with the outside world, I advise caution."

The elation in the room slightly died. While this did mean we could go out again, we could not go for a week or more without using our powers. A small throb moved through my left arm at the thought.

Despite this troubling addition when I looked over to Josh he was beaming. A light summer breeze was ruffling the hair of those directly around him.

"So we're going to be let out again. Finally," Merlin was chomping at the bit to get out of the base.

"Seems so," I agreed. "Where do you think we'll go next?"

"Mmmm... I'd like to go south again," a glazed daydreaming look filled his eyes, "Or Greece. We haven't been there yet and the islands sound amazing."

"And that has absolutely nothing to do with it's one of the oldest known cities ever," I added, knowing perfectly well he had a stack of books detailing the history of humanity next to his bedside.

Cyrus waved a hand in front of Merlin's face. "Don't get your hopes up. You know there's a mile-long list of chapters asking for help. You'll probably be sent around delivering jammers for a while."

136

I tilted my head slightly. "How many other bases are there exactly?"

"In our network? Twenty-seven," Cyrus rhymed off, "Though I think it's something like fifty-two in total."

My mouth parted slightly, "There are twenty-something independent bases?" I hadn't expected it to be that many. Maybe one or two.

"Oh no," Ember shook her head. "Only like five are independent. The others are part of their own networks. Like the Oceanic network. They have bases in Australia, New Zealand, Indonesia and Papua New Guinea."

Cyrus nodded along with his sister. "And those are just the ones we know about. Father expects there are at least another fifty. Maybe more."

I could only imagine what it would be like if we all joined together.

#

By the time we finished lunch and made our way back to the recruitment office, Josh was waiting for us. He was a jumping sack of glee. In his hand, he held one of the signal jammers. "This little gem is our ticket back out into the world." It didn't look like much up close. Just a simple box. Elleen was sitting behind Josh's desk assembling more of the little boxes.

Merlin reached over and picked up one of the jammers. "Did you make these Elleen?"

The small mousy-faced girl dropped her gaze to her work. "I just helped. It's nothing really."

"It's amazing is what it is!" Josh was practically dancing. "Which means I know where we're going next."

"And where is that?" I asked.

Josh picked up a letter from the teetering pile on his desk. "The London chapter has requested our help. Their base is below the Underground and they are trapped down there. Every time they move remotely close to the surface they set off a sensor. Several of their members have been captured. As soon as they are under the compulsion, they'll be able to lead New Atlantis to the others."

"So we need to get them out... do they know where they want to go?" Merlin held his hand out to see the letter. Josh handed it over.

I, in the meantime, grabbed an atlas and held it open to Great Britain.

"Somewhere out of the city." Josh leaned over my shoulder, looking at the map. "The letter says they would like to make a push for being self-sustained. So someplace with enough land to live on and cultivate. Far enough from the cities where they can be safe from the sensors."

Looking at the map, I saw that would be difficult. "There are a few national parks. Maybe there?"

"Maybe. They might have a plan as well. They know the area better than us after all and all our resources are from before the general fall of civilization."

#

It was good to have a goal again. We spent the rest of the day researching London in eager preparation, so we were all a little surprised when Josh announced that it was supper time.

In typical recruitment team fashion, all our books and notes were left right in the middle of the table in whatever state they were in when we finished working.

Merlin and I went back to the dining hall to find Ember and Cyrus already at our table. Ember was sporting her trademark grin.

"Evening," I said somewhat cautiously.

"How was work?" Cyrus asked, also seeming rather chipper.

"Amazing!" Merlin sat down beside his roommate. "We're going to London in a few days."

"That was quick." Though, Cyrus didn't sound a bit surprised in the least. "No wonder Josh looked so happy at the announcement."

"We should do something tonight," Ember was all but bouncing in her seat. "Let's go into the mansion. To the ballroom or the solarium."

I blinked, a little surprised, "Ah... sure. Why not."

"Let's make a stop in the library as well," Merlin added, and I just knew he wanted to poke around for books on English history.

"Yes, yes of course," Ember waved her hand. Despite the fact that we had just literally sat down for supper, Ember and Cyrus were, by this time, finished. Ember was already getting out of her seat, Cyrus quickly behind her. "Meet us there? Cy and I have some errands to run first," and without an ounce of elaboration, they left.

Merlin and I shared a single look that said exactly the same thing. After a long silence, Merlin shrugged and turned back to his meal, "I'm sure we'll find out what she's up to sooner or later. Sooner rather than later, knowing Ember."

We tossed some possibilities back and forth, each more ridiculous than the last. When we reached the point of speculating that Ember and Cyrus were planning to topple New Atlantis on their own and claim themselves as co-emperors of the world, we moved on to talking about London. Merlin had been there once before and told me all that he remembered about the place. The London chapter had command of the entire Underground with the entrances hidden all over the city. All the other entrances had been shut off years ago by New Atlantis before the chapter had been formed. They had a few trains still in operation they could use to go anywhere they wanted.

The base was sculpted into the earth under the Blackfriars station. They decided on that spot for two reasons; one that it was close to the city centre found at the Tower of London, and two if New Atlantis ever discovered it, it could be easily flooded by the River Thames. It was the safest way to guarantee they didn't hand over New Atlantis information on the other known bases to New Atlantis on a silver platter. The only problem was now it was a prison until they could get past the sensors.

After we finished our supper, Merlin and I strolled out into the hallway. We were about to turn towards the stairs leading up to the mansion above when a blank look crossed his expression, "Oh I forgot something in the office. Meet you upstairs in a minute?"

I shrugged and nodded, "Sure. I'll go check on the plants in the solarium then." There were sunflowers starting to bloom and herbs that needed cutting and drying.

"See you there," Merlin kissed my cheek and headed off down the hall. I went in the opposite direction for the stairs.

The hallways were always a swirl of activity in the evenings as most people had this time off. The mansion above was an entirely different atmosphere. The summer sun had not yet begun to set and light streamed in through the dust-streaked windows. Few people came upstairs for anything other than work.

On a whim, I took a different route towards the solarium. There were parts of the mansion that I had simply never bothered to explore before and I knew there was a service staircase somewhere near the kitchen. Now seemed as good a time as any to find it.

I was somewhere near the back end of the house when I heard a soft hum. My heart stopped for just a fraction of a second. It sounded like the essence engines from a New Atlantis vehicle, but after listening for a moment it wasn't exactly the same. This hum was deeper, a low rumble that didn't totally match the breathy hiss of essence engines.

I followed the sound into a large room that might have once been a parlour or a formal dining room. A crystal chandelier hung from the ceiling a Persian rug was laid out on the rich wooden floor. A green sofa was pushed up against one wall but that was all the remained of the original furniture.

My mouth went dry. I was not entirely wrong about the essence engines. The room housed an essence powered generator twice the size of me, a nearly empty tank of essence and a pod.

How could there be essence here? How could our generators be fuelled by it? Who was fuelling it? A churning feeling moved through my gut and I thought I might be sick. The taste of bile was sharp and bitter at the back of my throat.

My first instinct was to run. Did Marcus know? And if he did, how could he allow this? I could go to the dining hall downstairs and tell everyone we were being lied to. Our safe haven was powered by the very thing we sought to stop. The floor began to rumble as my mind crumbled under the uncontrolled questions that were swirling and swirling around as I backed into a corner, fists clenched tight.

A hiss joined the rumbling and the pod slid open. Of all the people, Marcus stepped out, looking exhausted. "Please don't do that Miss Chase," his tone was calm. He trudged to the couch and slumped down on it. For someone who had just stepped out of a pod, he still seemed himself nor did he seem bent on a murderous rampage.

My hands were fists at my sides, but by sheer force of will, the rumbling stopped.

"Thank you," he said in the same soft, calm tone. "The equipment is quite delicate."

My eyes were filling with angry red tears. "You've been lying to us. You... we trusted you!"

Marcus turned his tired eyes up at me. "And why can you no longer trust me?" He asked, more curious then defensive.

"Because that-" I thrust a finger towards the generator, "Is essence powered! You're using the very thing we are trying to stop to power this base! How many of us were used to fill that tank?!"

"None," Marcus answered simply. "It's all from me."

And with that, I stopped in my tirade feeling as if I had hit a brick wall.

Marcus gestured in the general direction of the equipment, "When I began the resistance, this was the technology that was readily available to me. It was what I knew well. There were other ways, solar power or wind, but they are inefficient and antiques."

I had no reply. There was a buzzing between my eyes stopping me from thinking properly.

Marcus sighed softly, "Utilizing essence is not the evil we are fighting Miss Chase. You use essence, after all, every time you use your powers. We fight against removing the essence entirely and with it a person's humanity. We fight against the compulsion and the thousands of people who are unknowing pawns for New Atlantis."

I swallowed hard, biting back the bitter taste. I wanted to believe him, I so wanted to believe him. "You... power it all yourself? But..."

"Essence is an incredibly efficient resource, Miss Chase," Marcus began to explain, "I need only to syphon some off every few days or so. So long as I rest and continue to use my powers, there are no lasting effects."

The world was spinning. The roiling feeling that I initially felt had turned to uncertainty. "How can you possibly use your powers? You're exhausted."

Marcus offered a small weak smile, "It gets easier." He stood and moved towards me. "Extraction can slow the spread of the disease but it doesn't stop it. Only using the powers does that." He stood in front of me, "If you have more questions drop by my office anytime. I am afraid at the moment I am not at my best. Though..." He looked at me straight in the eye, "I must ask that you don't tell others about this. It is within the nature of humanity to not always listen to reason."

I gave a small nod, the anger slowly easing away under the surface. At least, I didn't feel like causing it to disappear down a deep black hole anymore. I wasn't sure what to think myself, but he obviously wasn't in any condition to talk about it right now. "Do Ember and Cyrus know?"

Marcus made a small noise in his throat. "They do. Ember helps maintain the equipment, and Cyrus put himself in charge of my health." His brows furrowed, "They have offered to share the burden but I will not allow it. They need their strength more than I."

There was a strange note in his voice. Like tenderness mixed with urgency. "I won't say anything. Although I may have more questions later." Once I had time to think and get the conflicting opinions in order. It was simply the principle of it that I didn't like. If I was honest with myself, I knew that Marcus wasn't hurting anyone. He was only doing all he could for the people in his care.

"Of course," Marcus nodded. "Now then, you should go Miss Chase. Ember and Cyrus are likely out of their meeting now and they will have some news to share." He moved past me and began his way down the hall.

"What kind of news?" I called back, but he merely waved and kept walking.

Perplexed, conflicted, and curious, I closed the door of the generator room and went in search for Ember, Cyrus, and Merlin, doing my best not to stumble on any more secrets along the way. I heard them before I saw them. Ember was softly humming in the ballroom and her feet were tapping against the marble floor. When I walked in, she was dancing the waltz with an invisible partner. Cyrus and Merlin were standing off to the side in animated conversation.

"Am I late?"

Ember pirouetted around to face me with the biggest grin on her face. "Not at all. We just got here ourselves," she skipped closer. Her smile faded. "Terra? You look like you've seen a ghost."

Evidently, I wasn't as calm as I thought I was. I pushed a smile, uncertain if it looked at all genuine, "It's alright. It just... had a little chat with your Dad in the generator room."

A silent conversation moved between the three of them, including Merlin, much to my surprise. "Terra it's not..." Merlin began before I waved my hand to stop him.

143

"It's alright. Marcus explained it," I couldn't help but narrow my eyes slightly. "Though it might have come as less of a shock if someone thought to tell me."

"It never came up," Cyrus answered honestly. "That, and well, think of it from our perspective. When you first came you were traumatized. You were taken directly from a pod. You had just lost a friend. If you had known about the generators from the beginning, you would have never given us a chance."

I crossed my arms, unable to argue with that logic. "But what about after?"

"As I said, it never came up."

Ember pouted. "Oh, Terra. We're sorry. Truly but Father made us promise not to tell anyone unless we needed to."

"They were much more secretive about it before," Merlin mused. "I badgered Cyrus for weeks before he told me anything. He kept sneaking off and insisted it was more practice."

Ember took both of my hands. "Forgive us?"

In spite of how I felt a giggle burst past my lips, "You look like a squirrel when you make that face," and she hugged me, the droop in her shoulders disappearing in an instant. "Now then, you had news?" I prompted, having no desire to stay on that topic for the time being.

Ember released me and her grin turned sheepish. She looked to Cyrus who simply nodded, then she took a breath, "We're joining the recruitment team!"

My jaw dropped. I looked to Merlin who had a mirrored expression, "But... how... what?"

The Cheshire grin crept back onto Ember's lips. "What with everything going on in the world, we thought Josh could use some extra hands. So we asked Father if we could transfer."

Cyrus crossed his arms. "He wasn't certain at first. It's dangerous work. But we convinced him that it was what we wanted."

Ember's hands were beginning to move as she talked. "We had our meeting with Josh after supper. He had to agree before it's official. After we explained our motives, he thought we would be good additions to the team so... we're in!"

A long silence stretched out before us. Merlin nor I had any idea how to reply. Ember's shoulders began to droop again. "You... don't think we should?" she asked tentatively.

I blinked and broke out of my silence, "N-no that's - that's wonderful Ember!" I pulled her into a tight embrace while Merlin clapped Cyrus on the shoulder.

"Are you coming to London then?" Merlin asked, tilting his head slightly.

"Seems so. You know Josh, he's a little anxious sending us out so soon, but it's not like we're new to the resistance. He's going to need all hands on deck."

The rest of the evening was spent talking about Ember and Cyrus' new position, and about the upcoming mission, even though they would be coming to the office with us in the morning. Long after the sun began to set, we moved up to the solarium and continued to talk. Merlin and I curled together on the wicker settee watching the stars blooming above us. The knowledge of the generators was still clinging to the back of my mind. I still didn't like it, but it was Marcus' sacrifice, not mine, towards the greater good.

CHAPTER TWELVE

Into the Underground

The day of departure was much the same as Quebec. We rose early and met just outside the vehicle hanger. Arthur had the plane ready to go, supplies were packed and we began our long flight across the ocean.

When we arrived the skies were ink black. Only a few stars could be seen through the thick cover of clouds.

Arthur landed on a strip of old highway. Our particular section was pristine, but one glance at the side roads and it was easy to see that this was the only usable chunk of road for miles.

"Where does Arthur hide the plane?" I looked to Merlin as he had been here before.

"Technically he doesn't." Merlin handed me my bag, "He'll just leave it sprawled out in the middle of the road and he has a story to tell curious people. I can't remember the exact details but it has something to do with a wealthy patron sending him to get things and an emergency landing."

I blinked, not understanding, "But wealth is useless these days." Most people still had a little money stashed away. My parents had a safe at home filled with useless paper.

"Money wealth sure," Cyrus joined in, shouldering his bag, "But so long as there are people on this earth, someone will find a way to feel superior."

"Hey guys, gather round," Josh called us over to form a loose circle, "Now remember the London chapter have control of the underground. One of their sympathetics is meeting us under the Chesham station." He then pulled out a bag of jammers, "Everyone take one. Remember that it's powered by your baseline essence. No need to turn it on or anything like that. I want you all to keep one with you at all times."

I took a jammer and slipped it in my pocket before taking Merlin's hand. The jammers were only designed to shield one person at a time. When we tested them at the base, they could sometimes cover two, but only if both people were calm and recently used their powers beforehand. So with only twenty jammers, we planned to move the London chapter out in groups.

#

It was a little under an hour to get from the plane to Chesham station.

"See that building over there?" Merlin pointed out a tiny stone building at the end of the lane on which we stood. "That's the old Chesham station entrance."

We did not go that way. We turned right, going down a small hill and stopping outside a red brick building with a peeling blue door. The sign outside said it was once a music store.

The door was not locked. We walked in, Josh leading the way towards the back of the shop. A cluttered mess of instruments, chairs, and stacks of papers surrounded us. It was hard to believe that this was once a functioning business.

If you looked closely, there was a path through the rubble. It led directly back to a blank stretch of wall made from the same red brick as the rest of the building.

"Terra? Would you mind?" Josh gestured to the blank stretch of wall.

Stepping forward, I touched my hand against the wall. The bricks shifted and turned outward, creating an arch. The now open

148

passage led down to a staircase. I had a feeling the stairs were made by a fellow earth elementalist as the steps appeared to be made from a solid piece of stone.

"Watch your heads," Josh cautioned and ducked down the steps. Ember and Elleen held balls of flames in their hands to light our way. Kalle closed the entrance behind us.

It was dark until the very bottom where electric lights spilt their incandescence across the station platform. As promised, a train was waiting for us.

Two young men were waiting on the platform. Upon seeing us, the taller one nudged the smaller and they both turned to face us, "Long walk Josh?" the taller of the two men asked.

"Looks like there's more of you this time. New recruits?" The smaller eyed us over. The pair reached out to shake Josh's hand in welcome and then the rest of us in turn.

"We have one newish recruit. New to you at least. Terra joined us last fall." Josh gestured to me, and then to Cyrus and Ember, "Cyrus and Ember are transfers. Terra, Cyrus, Ember, this is Eric and Charlie. They operate the train."

"A pleasure," replied Charlie.

Without further adieu, Eric glanced at an antique pocket watch, "Best be on our way. The others will be getting anxious."

Charlie and Eric got in the control booth of the train and opened the passenger doors for us. "Mind the gap!" Eric warned with a barking laugh.

#

From Chesham station, it was the metropolitan line to Finchley Road. We switched to the Jubilee line to Westminster station, and finally, we took the District line to Blackfriars.

The station was as empty and nondescript as the others. Faded movie posters and shattered advertisements decorated the space. The

149

base was supposedly around here somewhere, but the location didn't exactly jump out at you.

"Right this way ladies and gentlemen." Eric and Charlie corralled us to a set of benches. They knocked on the bricks and at once the wall opened up to another passage of descending steps.

"How do they know it's us on the other side of the wall?" I whispered to Merlin. I considered what Josh had said when we were still preparing for this mission. Somewhere, some of the London members were being cured. How was the base not discovered if one simply needed to knock on the wall to get in?

"There's a pattern in the knock. It changes every couple days." Merlin explained. "And look... mmm... there. See the camera?" He pointed to a far corner of the platform.

I did indeed. It was fastened to a wall with tendrils of stone.

Merlin began his way down the steps, "Though all the secrecy in the world doesn't stop a sledgehammer. If New Atlantis knew where to go, they could force their way in. All this just protects them from being found by accident."

We descended into the brightly lit caverns of Blackfriars base. There was an element of pride and craftsmanship in how the base was built. The walls were a rainbow of marble and coloured glass. Frescos were carved into the walls using the colours to paint panoramic scenes across every surface.

"Charlie!" Eric nudged his partner, "I'm going to go tell the girls that they're here. You show them to their rooms?"

A nod was exchanged and Eric disappeared. I was bone tired and made no protest to being led down more of the beautiful corridors. The soft sound of snoring could be heard behind some of the other doors along the way. Charlie stopped and gestured to three identical doors on a wall of birds flying through the mountains, "These are your rooms. It's four to a room. The toilet is that red door at the end of the hall."

Josh gave a little nod, "Thank you, Charlie."

150

Charlie bobbed his head and left.

Josh turned to us, "You all get some rest. Tomorrow will be a long day without a doubt."

No one was in the state to argue. Ember, Cyrus, Merlin and I shuffled to the same room. Our sleeping quarters were simply furnished with two sets of bunk beds. I was pleased to see that the frescos continued into the bedrooms.

Ember and I went to one bunk where I was happy to sleep on the bottom. Ember yawned above me and I felt the bed move as she found a comfortable position, "They have a nice place here. The walls are so pretty."

"Yeah..." I murmured in agreement, rolling towards the wall. I touched a finger against the cool stone, "Maybe we should try to convince your Dad to let us spruce up home a little bit."

"I don't know about the whole base," Cyrus' voice came from the top bunk on his and Merlin's side of the room, "But ask him about the dining hall. It's a community area after all."

I smiled to myself, thinking of a little more colour and beauty in the normally sterile metallic structure that was our home. "Maybe..." I whispered and pulled my hand away. In the space where my thumb was, there was now a tiny tree that looked like it had always been a part of the whimsical landscape.

#

No one came to wake us the next morning. I felt the groggy pull of oversleep as I made my way down to breakfast with the others. At once I noticed that most of the London chapter was already finished and were gone to start their day. The cook was kind enough to leave out extra for us, even asking if we wanted anything else made once the dishes were cleared. I was happily sipping a cup of real English tea when two young women came to join us.

They were about my age. One of the girls wore her hair in a rocker style bob the exact colour of fire. The colour flickered as she moved, shifting from the deepest reds to brightest yellows with

151

sometimes just a hint of blue. The other girl looked, in a word, ethereal. Her eyes were the colour of a dawn sky. Her waist length brown hair and the hem of her white lace dress fluttered in an unseen breeze.

"Everyone, this is Kay and Charlotte." Josh gestured first to the girl with the hair of fire, and then to the ethereal girl. "They are the current acting leaders of the London chapter."

"Hello." I murmured, echoing the other's replies. Only Cyrus didn't immediately respond, a frown blossoming between his brows, "What happened to David?"

Kay's lips pressed into a hard line as Charlotte addressed the question, "He was captured."

My gut twisted. "Doesn't that mean..."

Charlotte nodded, "We expect he'll lead New Atlantis here the moment he's cured. We've alerted the chapters in Scotland and Northern France as well. They are thankfully the only ones he ever visited personally."

"But what about the others?" Cyrus' concern for our own home was evident, "Did he know the location of any others?"

"No," Kay answered much to the relief of everyone. "We keep that information secret from even ourselves. And besides, even if he marched in here today we've destroyed most of the records." Kay grinned with the tiny victory.

Though despite their efforts to protect everyone else, they were still trapped. I shifted in my seat feeling the soft weight of the jammer in my pocket. I watched as Josh pulled out his own and showed it to Charlotte and Kay, "With this, you'll soon be safe too."

He explained what the box did, much to their fascinated expressions. "I'm afraid we only had time to make twenty. We'll have to move you in groups. But Marcus promises to send more as they can be made." Josh slipped the tiny box back into his pocket, "On that note, do you have any idea where you would like to go?"

The girls looked at each other. I had the notion that they had discussed that very question in length already, "There is a place." Charlotte began, "Thorpe Park. It's on an island, sort of."

Josh tilted his head. Thorpe Park had never come up during our brief research. "Can you show us where it is?" He asked.

"Sure." Kay motioned for us to follow, "There's a map in the office."

#

It was sort of an island. There was a road that led into it though Charlotte and Kay assured us that that entire area had never been redeveloped by New Atlantis yet. Before the riots, it had been an amusement park. I wondered what such a thing must have been like.

"It's awfully close to the airport," I pointed out. While I doubted you would be able to see the park from the airport or vice versa, I was thinking of the supply planes flying over at night.

We were in the base's main office. It was a large room with the same carved stone walls. A fire was burning in a fireplace and Kay was periodically adding paper to the blaze. I wondered absently where the smoke went.

"It's far enough for the sensors." Kay reached into the fire and stirred the ashes to encourage the papers to burn. "And as we said, there are no homes for miles."

I traced the island with the tip of my finger. It could be the perfect place really. Less than a day's journey from the city, but far enough away that they could hide without being underground. So long as they were careful.

Beside me, Merlin cracked his knuckles. So much like his element, he didn't like staying still for long. "Let's go check it out." A murmur of agreement circulated among us. It wasn't as if we had all the time in the world after all.

Josh smiled at the enthusiasm. He turned to Charlotte and Kay, "How long would it take to get there?"

153

"The Underground will go as far as Richmond station." Charlotte began, pointing out the spot on the map.

Kay tilted her head back and forth, "From there it's a... about four hours walk. So give five hours for the entire trip one way."

Josh looked over his shoulder at us. "Merlin, Terra, Cyrus and Ember. Why don't you go?" He suggested. "The rest of us will remain here to investigate any other leads and help pack up."

"I'll go too." Kay stepped forward, but not without looking to her partner, "Charlotte? Hold the fort?"

"Be careful," Charlotte said softly. Even her voice sounded like the wind. I wondered if that was her mark. Not anything you could see, just a presence. "Have Eric take you."

The hum of activity settled on the group. Kay came over to Josh and held out a hand, "I'm going to need one of those jammers though."

"Of course," Josh reached in his pocket and put his own jammer in her hand, "Safe travels."

#

The journey to Thorpe Park was uneventful. Eric brought us as far as Richmond station. He promised to be waiting for us tomorrow. With it already being near noon, we agreed that it would be best to spend the night in the park.

We made it there in good time following an old broken highway southwest. Charlotte and Kay had been right about one thing, there was no one around for miles. If Thorpe Park turned out to be a good place, they would have a good buffer between them and the city.

We stood at the southern edge of the Park. Once upon a time, there was a path called the "Monk's Walk' that included a bridge across the water. That bridge had long ago fallen into the mud and watery vegetation.

Cyrus simply leapt over to the island with the push of winds behind him. Merlin put his hands in his pockets and strolled across the water's surface as if the road never ended. He stopped midway across, waving at Ember, Kay, and I, "Well? What are you waiting for?"

With a faint giggle, I lifted a hand and a crude stone bridge began to span between the two shores. "Isn't it somewhat blasphemous to walk on water on the Monk's walk?" I mused once we had reached the other shore.

"Perhaps only a little." Merlin chirped and laced his hand in mine.

Walking into the park, we were first met by several small brown buildings all sitting around a spinning train ride.

"Do you think any of the rides still work?" Ember bounced around the trains with their colourful albeit peeling paint.

Cyrus tried a couple door handles. Some were rusted or broken enough that he was able to poke his head in the small brown buildings. He glanced back at his sister. "Probably not, but you could probably fix them Em."

We continued further in the park. After we passed the fourth or so restaurant, Cyrus nudged his head towards the sign and said, "You'll be at no lack for kitchen equipment. There should be enough in these buildings for what you need plus spare parts."

"And it already has a toilet." Merlin provided helpfully, hitching his thumb at a building with a large sign that read 'Toilets'. I gave him a soft nudge In the ribs for that.

"Plenty of open space as well." I added, perhaps a little more helpfully then Merlin, "Lots of room for a garden.

Kay did not say much as we explored. She was quiet, calculating as if she were weighing every pro and con in her mind.

At one point Merlin's eyes widened with delight, "Is that..." He tugged on my hand, pulling me toward what could only be described as a giant metallic shark. Lines of rust made it look wounded. The sign on the outside stated that it was the hotel.

"Well, that's living quarters taken care of." He was beaming, "I would gladly sleep in a shark."

There was another gem waiting for us. When we were wandering the water park, Ember noticed the medical centre. A quick look inside, and we were shocked to see many of the medical supplies were still there. Somehow untouched by the riots.

"My word." I gasped softly, holding a tiny vial of liquid as if it were as precious as gold. "Penicillin." How could this all just go unnoticed?

Once we had walked the entirety of the park, we came back to the southern end. We sat beneath the canopy of benches arranged like covered wagons. The particular one where we were sitting still had its canopy mostly intact. Only a few spots of pure sunlight beamed in on the softer golden shade.

We sat down to eat the little food we brought with us for supper. Not until the last crumbs did Cyrus finally venture to ask the question that was on all our minds, "So, what do you think?" He asked Kay.

Kay looked over her shoulder, not answering for several long seconds as if formulating the last of her answer, "It needs some work. But it'll do. That hotel would house everyone without having to expand."

"And it's in a shark!" Merlin added as if that made all the difference.

Kay smiled, and gave a little shrug, "All of the other places we were considering would never be as well equipped as this; housing, kitchens, lands, even medical equipment. The only concern really is the airport. We won't be able to have lights at night. Someone flying over may see."

"So..." I laced my fingers together on the table, "Do you think you'll stay?"

With a firm nod, Kay smiled. Her hair literally glowed in the dimming sun. "I think so." She stood, "Let's go take inventory. Cyrus and

Merlin, would you be willing to find what kitchen equipment still works? Ember would you come with me to sort out some rooms in the shark. And Terra, Josh said you help with the gardens at home. Would you start clearing a patch of land?"

"Sound like a plan." I beamed, and we head out.

CHAPTER THIRTEEN

Past, Present, and Future

We returned the next day with the good news. Josh and Charlotte were so excited that the rooms filled with a chipper summer breeze.

"We don't have enough jammers to cover everyone at once." Josh reminded Kay and Charlotte. They were beginning to plan out how best to move everything and everyone.

"Yes of course. It will have to be done in groups." Charlotte agreed, "Some of our sympathetics are in the market buying seeds. As soon as they are back we will decide who to send on the first trip."

It was decided that most of the sympathetics and as many Tellurians as the jammers could cover would go on the first trip. It was agreed that with every trip, four of our group would go along for extra help and to bring the jammers back. As Tasha, Braxton, Simon, and Edgar were going on the first trip, that meant twenty Tellurians from the London group were able to go first along with twelve sympathetics. Despite the risk of going in a larger group, it would mean more hands to begin repairs and rehabilitation of Thorpe Park. More beds could be sorted, the garden could be planted and the kitchen finished. Merlin and Cyrus had already identified what worked and what didn't, and the chosen kitchen was emptied and cleaned. It was just a matter now of putting everything where it belonged.

Those of us not going on that first trip stayed in the base. We packed up the essentials and destroyed everything else. As rooms were cleared, the stone was filled back into a natural formation.

Ember, Merlin, Cyrus and I were due to go on the last trip to Thorpe Park. When we asked how long it would be to get back to the plane from the park, Josh told us that Arthur was working on moving the plane closer to the park. If all went well, it would only be a short journey.

Nearly a week had passed. Everything that needed packing was gone or waiting. Everything else was destroyed. I still didn't know where all the smoke went. If New Atlantis decided to appear the last couple days, there would be nothing to find other than empty rooms.

Kalle, Elleen, Frank, and Josh returned by lunchtime. Everything that remained was loaded onto the train for the last journey in the morning. After everyone was in Thorpe Park, we only planned to stay another couple days at most. Kalle had left to meet up with Arthur to help with any difficult spans of the road.

With nothing else to do, Ember, Merlin, Cyrus and I were playing cards in the dining hall. "We should do something," Ember said, throwing down yet another winning hand. "If it's our last night in the city, we should go see a castle or something."

"You can't get any closer to Buckingham Palace than the front gate." Cyrus reminded his sister, "Rumour is that the remaining members of the royal family are in there. They don't have any power now, but there're enough monarchists in England that having the last members of the royal family under your thumb would be helpful."

Ember sent a spark at her brother, "You sound just like Father when you talk like that. Where's your sense of adventure?"

Cyrus blew out of the spark before it hit him.

"Why not Tower Bridge?" Merlin suggested, "It's close. And we should be able to see the Tower of London without getting too deep in the crowds." Neither Merlin nor I were particularly enthusiastic to go into another market after what happened in Quebec.

"Might I suggest..." Charlotte had entered the room in that floating sort of walk of hers, "St. Paul's Cathedral? It's quite beautiful and open to the public."

A grin spread on Merlin's face, "Oh yes. Let's do both." In a moment, he was on his feet, "Did you want to come with us Charlotte? Or Kay if she's not busy."

Charlotte smiled a soft ethereal smile, "No thank you. You have fun. Josh is in the office with the jammers."

We got up, excited to have a diversion for the rest of the day. "Well... thanks!" Merlin waved as we left.

#

London has a reputation of being permanently under a cloud. On this particular day, the sun was just poking out from the grey sky and the air was warm with a gentle breeze. After days underground, I relished the air and light.

"I wish our base was like Thorpe Park." I murmured, stepping onto the cracked pavement with Merlin's hand in mine.

"Do you even notice the difference?" Cyrus asked with a chuckle, "You spend more time outside then the gardeners."

"That's only because we train outside." I countered though I knew it to be true. I felt too confined underground, within my element or not. I understood the necessity of it, but still.

"We could probably live above ground." Merlin's voice was low as to not be overheard by the general public.

"How?"

"Well..." he reached up and scratched the back of his head, "The base is on a huge plot of land. There is a city just beyond the woods, but we could easily hide a cabin or two maybe."

Cyrus sighed softly, "Father would never allow it." I tried not to feel too crestfallen, "The more we branch out, the more chance we have of being caught. Even the gardens outside took some convincing. But thankfully the greenhouses alone couldn't feed everyone."

I shuddered at the idea of not even having that small escape, "What about the recruitment team?"

161

"Well..." Cyrus's own voice dropped as we began the ascent up Tower Hill. Despite being some ways from the market, the streets were thick with people, "Josh made a good argument. Father wanted to keep training contained underground. But Josh argued that it would only be for an hour or two at most daily. That and his team needed experience out in the elements." A crooked grin pulled at the edge of Cyrus' lips, "Not to mention it would look pretty silly if the entire recruitment team were pale as ghosts even in the middle of summer."

A giggle burst from my lips. The idea of the perpetually tanned Merlin being pale was mildly hilarious. Unlike Ember, who had an ivory completion no matter how long she waited in the sun.

We were forced to end the conversation as we arrived at the edge of the marketplace. Opting not to go into the market itself, we walked along the outskirts. Merlin was ringing with a list of notable historical figures who were held prisoner in the Tower of London; the nine days queen Lady Jane Grey, the second wife of King Henry XIII Anne Boleyn, and the boy princes Richard and Edward who disappeared from history in their childhood. Merlin mentioned a few others I didn't recognize and could not later recall.

After the market, we walked towards the aptly named Tower Bridge. Two towers stood guard on either shore, supporting the bridge between them. It certainly was something. We opted not to stay long. Even by the bridge, the crowd was a hive.

St. Paul's Cathedral was in the entirely opposite direction. On the way, Merlin insisted that we take the slight detour to pass the monument to the great fire of London. Once upon a time, you could climb to the top of the monument and look over the city. New Atlantis had since boarded up the entrance, deeming it unsafe for the time being.

Finally, we made it to one of the few landmarks in the city that were still being cared for, St. Paul's Cathedral. Walking in it was just breathtaking. I never saw anything like it before. The mosaic tiled floor was polished to a shine and reflected the light of a thousand flickering candles. The air was warm and heavy, but not unpleasantly so. Tattered leather bound bibles were left on the scrubbed wooden pews.

I did not understand faith myself. It was not something I was raised with though I knew it brought comfort to some. We were not alone in the church. Others were sitting quietly in the pews, consulting the black leather books, or lighting the candles at the periphery of the hall. Whatever it was that they were seeking in this place, I hoped they found it.

As I was walking around admiring the artwork that someone must have painstakingly kept in good condition, I noticed Ember and Cyrus lighting one of the candles. Ember's mouth moved in soft words before she and Cyrus made an identical motion in front of them with their hands.

I gave Merlin's hand a little squeeze, "What are they doing?" I asked, curious. Ember and Cyrus were leaving the candles to look around.

"Lighting a candle for their mother."

When I just gave him a blank look he smiled gently.

"I take it your family wasn't any sort of religious?"

I shook my head, "Not particularly no."

Merlin led me over to the candles, "Every lit candle is a prayer. That's how Cyrus explained it to me at least. He said that his mother would light a candle every night for the sick. After she fell ill herself, they kept it up as long as they could."

"Do they still?" I gazed over the hundreds of flickering prayers.

"When they can." Merlin gave a little shrug, "I used to bring back candles when I could find them."

"Hey, guys." Ember and Cyrus had come back to us, "What's next? I suppose we can't be out much longer."

After a moment of thought, my eyes lit with a memory from a sleepover another lifetime ago, "How about the Globe Theatre? I heard they were rebuilding it."

We stepped out into the grey sunshine. Merlin put an arm over my shoulders, "Why not. If we're lucky maybe they'll be rehearsing something. Arthur would be so jealous if we told him we saw a snippet of a live Shakespearean production."

I gave the cathedral one last lingering look, "I would love to catch a few lines of Hamlet. That was my Mom's favourite." There was a sudden pang in my heart, one that came so often that I didn't react outwardly to it. I wondered how my parents were, what they would think if they saw my life now. I knew they visited England in the early days of their marriage, likely they would have barraged me with nostalgia. Or at least, that was what they would have done before they were cured. I tried not to think about how they had worked with New Atlantis to try and find me when I first left.

We made a lingering way back to Blackfriars. The theatre was on the other side of Blackfriars bridge. I scanned the distant shoreline, trying to see the Globe Theatre before we had even reached the bridge. Ember was just behind me, reciting her favourite lines from Romeo and Juliet.

Wailing sirens punctuated the moment like a knife.

"Run!" Cyrus ordered us into motion.

We raced for the bridge. Half a dozen vans were haphazardly parked around the old entrance to Blackfriars Station. My powers reached for the earth below us, "Get ready for stairs!" I shouted, and the street opened up, sweeping downwards towards the platform below.

The platform was pandemonium.

New Atlantis officers outnumbered the remains of the base two to one. Josh, Charlotte and Kay were struggling to hold back the officers as the others got on the train. The train seemed to be the officer's focus, rather than the people themselves. No doubt they were tipped off that the trains worked now.

My gut clenched when I realized that some of the officers were not uniform. They were the captured London chapter members, cured and returned.

As we got closer, Cyrus sent a gust of wind to knock back the officers. There wasn't a clear divide between officers and resistance. Ember hung back, afraid to burn anyone by accident. I did the same, preferring not the skewer anyone on our side.

Josh, Charlotte and Kay were standing in front of a wall of fire that blocked the entrance to the train. Frank was helping people inside with water bubbles.

Nearest to the front, one of the newly cured was trying to talk to Kay and Charlotte. By then I was close enough to hear a bit of the conversation, "Kayleigh. Charlotte. Please, stop this madness. We were wrong about the cure. We were blind and mislead. It's safe. Please." The man reached out a hand to them, "I'm still the same see. I'm still David."

"It's Kay you scrub." Kay bit out. Her hands filled with fire.

"David..." Charlotte's face was full of the bitter pain of betrayal, "You being here only proves that everything we believe was right." She lifted her hands. The winds plucked David and several of the officers into the air.

"You're not David," Kay added simply, and the swirling winds lit with fire.

I tried not to hear the screams. "Josh!" I called out, "What do you want us to do?"

He spared a glance for us, before knocking away more of the officers, "Merlin, Terra, flood what's left of the base. Everyone is out now. Ember, Cyrus, help Frank get everyone on the train."

A brief nod and we were off. With earth and water, Merlin and I knocked the officers away from the base entrance. I pulled a stone wall up to protect us, I was not keen on getting shot at again.

I stood on the first step that led down into the base. It was a shame to destroy it, but I understood the necessity. We didn't want to leave anything behind. We didn't want to give New Atlantis even an ounce of fuel. Touching the wall, I closed my eyes and felt through the earth. I felt the stone walls, the curve towards the dining hall, the wall of the kitchens. The river Thames was just beyond that. It was difficult to control something so far from myself, but I felt a crack in the stone and I willed it to spread. Little by little, inch by inch, the wall shattered.

"There." I breathed, "The water is coming now."

Merlin gently pulled me back, "You'll want to be out of the way for this. Drop the shield," he grinned. I could hear the water before I saw it. I shattered the stone wall and a wave rolled up onto the station and swept across the officers.

"Merlin! Terra! Hurry up!" Josh called from the train. Everyone was on board. Ember and Cyrus were waiting for us in the doors.

Merlin swirled water around us, picking up some of the rocks from the shattered shield wall in a vortex of stone and water to protect us. We were nearly at the train when the spindly sound of clanking metal came from the old station entrance.

We stopped dead. A machina, I only ever saw one on the news a lifetime ago. This one had eight long thin legs in a rolling motion around its central orb of a body.

"Shit." I hissed.

The machina made a beeline for the train. It wrapped it's long legs around the train and rocked it trying to haul it off the tracks.

A pillar of stone shot up and knocked one of the legs off the train. But it was only one leg, and it just returned to its prey, barely distracted. Ember and Cyrus ran over to us. A bolt of fire hit the machina directly in the body, nudging it but again barely distracting it.

I looked at Josh who waited in the open train doors, "Josh we'll knock it off." I screamed, "Go. We'll catch up." There was only a moment of hesitation. Or at least, that's all Josh had before one of the legs was reaching in the train. The doors closed on the appendage, cutting off the lower half.

166

Merlin, Ember, Cyrus and I stood together, "On the count of three." I said, "One, two, three, go!" A barrage of elements hit the machina at once. Pillars of stone rose up around the train, knocking off legs. Balls of fire pelted the body. Water and air came in at one side and knocked the machina off. I saw Eric and Charlie in the control booth mouth a 'good luck' before they slammed the train into motion.

The train slipped out of the station. That left us, thirty or so officers, and one hell of a giant angry spider remaining.

"Plan?" Cyrus asked and the winds picked up around us.

"Get out of the station and hide?" I suggested hopefully.

Merlin rolled his shoulders, "Short, sweet, and to the point. I like it."

The machina had rolled back up on its legs and started down the tunnel after the train. I pulled up a wall of stone as quickly as I could, sealing the way. On a thought, I started sealing the other ways out as well. I felt my breath growing ragged.

The entirety of the New Atlantis force turned on us then. Before they could start shooting, waves of water and air kept them from gaining footing while Ember single-handedly held back the machina.

I kept sealing off the ways until there was only one way out of the station, the stairs I made earlier to come in. "Get to the stairs. Once we're on the surface, I'll seal them in." I felt the deep throbbing ache in my arm, "After that...I probably won't be able to use my powers anymore."

Merlin gave a little nod, "Don't worry. We'll protect you." He said softly, taking my hand and giving it a little squeeze.

We edged towards the steps, not daring to turn our back on the New Atlantis horde. Ember formed a wall of fire to keep them from following us as we got the rest of the way up. I closed the way shut. There, they were trapped. Likely not for long, but long enough for us to get away.

I felt ready to collapse but forced my feet towards the bridge. Merlin pulled me along in the grey sunshine with Ember and Cyrus close in front of us.

The sirens that had been wailing all this time abruptly stopped once we were on the other end of the bridge. We turned left, running through a metal gate down a walking path along the waterfront.

"What now?" Ember was breathless, her face flushed. We slowed to a walk and she pinched her eyes between her fingers. I didn't want to know how badly they hurt after all the fire she used.

Cyrus looked around, "We need to get back into the underground. Least then we can walk to Richmond. Where's the closest station?"

I didn't know. I tried to feel for a hollow beneath the earth but my arm gave a sharp pang in protest. "Keep walking, we'll find a sign eventually." I breathed.

I looked up at the nondescript brown buildings on our right, and the water on the left. Far ahead I could see the smokey silhouette of Tower Bridge. "There was a station near the market. If nowhere else, we can go back there."

It was a good a plan as any. I trudged forward with Merlin's hand tight in my own. After brown buildings and an abandoned art gallery, I got to see just the edge of the white Tudor style building of the Globe Theatre before we heard the hum of essence engines. Merlin's grip on my hand tightened, and we kept walking as nonchalant as we could. They would just pass by. They had to. The only ones who knew what we looked like were trapped in the Blackfriars station.

Behind us was the squeal of tires. We stopped and looked back to see four officers running towards us. By instinct, I tried to use my powers, but all I received was another sharp pain in my arm. Guns pointed at us, there was the sound of shots, and my vision went black.

CHAPTER FOURTEEN

Earth, Air, Fire, and Water

My head was pounding. Someone was shaking my arm.

"Terra. Terra wake up. Please wake up."

I groaned softly and rolled towards Merlin's voice. "Go back to sleep Merlin," I murmured without opening my eyes.

He persisted in the shaking, "Terra you need to get up now." Merlin sounded slightly apologetic, but the sense of urgency still lingered at the edge of his tone.

I opened my eyes, looking up into his face. Immediately I was wide awake. He looked awful. His lip was broken and a bruise was blossoming over his eye. "Merlin, what happened?"

He touched his lip almost as though he forgot about it, "I was awake when they brought us in. Let's just say, I didn't go peacefully?" The corner of his mouth twisted into the grimace of a smile. "They shot us with sleeper darts."

The room wasn't cold but I shivered. It was a blank square of a room. Natural light filtered through a frosted window behind a set of bars. "Where are we?" I asked, standing to look at the window. I couldn't see through it.

"An island somewhere." Merlin watched my slow exploration of the room, "I think they called it Azores?" A groan pushed through his lips, "Ember and Cyrus are here too. The officers took them somewhere else."

I bit my lip. I had planned to escape through the window, but it looked like we were taking the route via solid door instead. I reached for the door, feeling the cool welcoming metal beneath.

"Terra don-"

My mind reached for the metal, to make the latches slide away. The moment I tried, something sharp stung through my mark. I touched it, confused. I couldn't still be tired, could I? Why couldn't I use my powers?

Sensing my confusion Merlin pulled me into his arms, "It's an injection they gave us. It blocks our powers. Believe me, I tried. I was trying to drown their heads in water bubbles when they gave me this." He indicated his lip.

We moved back to the corner of the blank room. I curled into Merlin's arms, trembling. "Is it a clinic?" The words were on my lips before I could stop them.

"I don't think so. If the meant to heal us, they would have just brought us to the clinic in London."

I ached to have my powers back. It would be so easy. We could just break out and hide. Merlin could probably hold us underwater until New Atlantis stopped searching. Another reach for the metal door and I felt the beginning of pinpricks in my arm. I laid my head against Merlin's chest, listening to the steady familiar beat under his shirt, "Do you know what's happened to Ember and Cyrus?"

"I wish." Merlin rested his chin on the top of my head, "I don't think they are in danger though. Ember struggled just as much as me and they didn't even try to hurt her. Cyrus was awake, but still too out of it to be any real help." I felt him hesitate. "The officers knew their names."

I gave a little jolt. What was that supposed to mean? Merlin touched my hand gently to calm me, "As soon as we can, we'll find them and we'll get out. I promise."

I gave a little nod, hoping that he was right.

We waited for a full day in that room. There were no lights, so at night we were left in total darkness. Neither of us had felt secure enough to sleep so we did it in shifts, watching over each other a few hours at a time until the dawn.

At some point, after the sky had lightened, food was pushed through a hole in the wall; fresh fruit, bread, and water. Merlin attempted to manipulate the water. There was a faint ripple of movement before he gripped his chest. After breakfast, two guards came to escort us to a bathroom. Once we were returned to our cell, one of the guards pressed a needle into our arms. By lunch, Merlin couldn't make the water ripple anymore.

By my estimation, it was at least an hour or so past noon when the door of our cell swung open and officers pulled us out. I assumed that we were just being taken to the bathroom again until we were led in the opposite direction.

"Where are you taking us?" I asked the officers, clenching my fists to keep myself from trying to fight them.

"Mr Wolfe has requested your audience." The officer to my left answered.

My heart beat in an uncomfortable staccato rhythm, "Nikolai Wolfe?"

"As I said. Mr Wolfe." The guard affirmed briskly.

A tiny hope filled my veins. Ember had said that he had been like an uncle to her and Cyrus. Maybe he merely meant to take them out of harm's way. Maybe they were being better cared for then Merlin and I. And maybe... just maybe... they were better equipt to find a way out.

The guards led us through a set of sliding double doors into another sterile white room. Tall windows filled the room with light. It was a cloudless day outside, the sun was refracting off the blue-green water. There was a view of the island in the distance.

"Terra!" Ember and Cyrus were being held on a couch by a pair of guards. Neither were visibly bound, though as Ember began to get up to come to me, her guard grabbed her by the arm and hauled her back down.

"Em-" I took a step towards her before I too was shoved back.

"Now now now. Don't be hasty." The voice came from a man who looked unlike anyone I ever saw before. Both horrible and mesmerizing, he looked like fire. His skin was charred black though you could hardly see it beneath the glow of fire. His entire body burned just under the flesh, the flames following his movement like nervous impulses. As such, his face was always aglow with undulating light. His eyes were the brightest spots. Just white fire with no pupils. I knew he could see though. He was looking straight at Merlin and me.

"Gentlemen. Please show our guests to a seat."

Merlin was shoved towards the couch while I was brought closer to the fire man. He stepped aside, revealing a pod behind him. My conviction to not fight broke in that moment and I dug in my heels. "N-no!" A hand wrapped in my hair, pulling my head back as I was forced towards the pod. They lifted me and deposited me on the equipment, making quick work of the straps that bound wrists and ankles.

"Terra!"

I craned my head to see Merlin fighting with the guards, two were holding him down.

The fire man approached. Red-orange lips pulled back against a set of blackened teeth, "Terra Chase is it? A pleasure. I am Nikolai Wolfe."

I was hardly paying attention to him. I strained against the straps, pulling for my element in desperation. I gasped as white-hot pain seared through my arm.

"Tut tut tut. None of that now." Nikolai waved a finger at me as if speaking to a naughty child, "You feel that pain in your mark? It's a new invention of mine. A cocktail to block the expression of Telluria. I've been told it can be quite painful if you fight it. Quite the sophisticated bark collar no?"

He was looking at me, expecting an answer. Just looking at me. I couldn't read the expression on that burning face. Taking a breath, I willed myself to calm down. I felt the weight of my jade pendant against my throat, like Merlin said once before, a tiny earthen anchor to cling to when I needed it. After a moment, I met his unfailing gaze, "Why are we here?" I asked, managing much to my surprise to only sound curious. "If you intended to cure us then why not just leave us in London."

Nikolai stepped back and gave an exasperated sigh, "Because Miss Chase the cure isn't perfect. Despite whatever reputation proceeds me, I have little desire to turn my niece and nephew into one of those puppets." There was a mix of bitter and sweet in his voice. "It was only Ember and Cyrus I wanted of course, however... when my officers told me that they captured two of their friends as well, I found myself provided with a singularly interesting opportunity. In the matters of both espionage, and scientific curiosity."

I pulled at the bonds again, testing their strength. I suddenly wished I had fought just a little harder before being placed in the pod. "We would never help you." I hissed.

He raised an eyebrow, "Is that so?" He moved to the foot of the pod, "I do not remember offering a choice, Miss Chase."

A panic crawled up my throat. Nikolai touched the controls and the pod slid closed. All I could hear was muffled screaming and the pound of my heartbeat. The pod hummed to life. At once the opalescent gas filled the pod and I felt the bone-deep weakness settling in. Was he really doing this? After his speech about using us and the imperfect cure, was this really happening? There was no stone shard in the pod this time to cut my bonds.

Just as the stars began to form in my eyes, the machine hissed and opened. Nikolai was standing over me with an eager gaze. I was too weak to feel any particular fear from it. "I believe Miss Chase, that you were saying that you would not willingly help me. But you see, I do not ask for the things I want. I take." Nikolai put his hand on my wrist, taking note of my pulse. I struggled to just keep my eyes open.

As he looked down at me, his expression softened, "Understand Miss Chase that my only desire in this world is to see the end of this horrible disease. You can trust me on that fact can't you?"

Through slitted eyes, I gazed up at him. Or rather, I watched the inferno burning under his skin. "Yes."

He smiled without a hint of malice, "Just imagine it, a world without Telluria. It would become as mythical as smallpox. You want that too don't you Miss Chase?"

"Yes," I whispered again.

He moved somewhere to the region of my head. I heard the clink of glass and metal. "Marcus' resistance, while you lot mean well, are highly misguided. In an effort to stop my cure, you are hindering my work. I am afraid that unless the resistance is disbanded, I may die before a true cure can be discovered. You don't want that do you, Miss Chase?"

I remained silent. The resistance was good. I knew that. I had seen the good they do. "Wh-what about...the powers. Th-they-"

Nikolai's mouth pressed into a hard line. "Yes, they suspend your illness. But my personal beliefs aside, is it not like handing a child a loaded gun?" Nikolai's mouth twisted, "You cannot tell me that everyone in your resistance is as... talented... as you. Are there no accidents? I know that my darling Ember was personally responsible for nearly burning down her father's house twice when the powers were discovered."

I said nothing. He was right, again. The powers weren't always safe. I nearly killed Cyrus when I was just learning.

"Miss Chase? I'm afraid I didn't hear you."

I grit my teeth, frustrated at my lack of ability to think up a reply. All I wanted to do was close my eyes and pretend this wasn't happening.

174

"Uncle." Cyrus' voice came from the couch. "No, the powers are not always safe. But we have specialized rooms and trainers to contain any accidents. It's the same as learning any skill. There is always some risk-"

"Silence Cyrus." Nikolai's voice held a quiet power. "I have already told you my beliefs on the matter."

"But Uncle-" It was Ember this time, and I saw a blur of red hair struggling to stand. "And we have told you ours. Most in the resistance would rather die than take the cure. Is it not better to prolong their life until a true cure can be made?" Ember was pleading with him.

I suddenly understood why Nikolai was a man of fire. Despite having Telluria, he was not using his powers. But no one would have lasted this long just waiting. I thought back to Marcus' explanation of using the pod to only drain some of the essence away. It could prolong your life, but the mark would continue to grow.

"Why don't you use your powers?" I couldn't help but ask. "Draining little by little obviously isn't working well for you. You would have more time if you just-"

Nikolai stood over me. Something was in his hand though I couldn't see what. "The powers are not ours to use Miss Chase." He said softly. He closed his eyes, and for a moment I thought he might weep, but when he opened his eyes again they were filled with steel. "The earth is dying. This-" He gestured to his general form, "Is our punishment from the Earth for lifetimes of sin. Telluria is not the disease Miss Chase, we are. Telluria is merely the fever meant to wipe us out." He lifted his hand, revealing a syringe filled with a clear liquid. It resembled oil in water. He pushed the needle of the syringe against my arm. "My work is not to heal us, but to heal Gaia herself." He pushed down the plunger.

I shuddered, feeling a sensation like ice sweep through my right arm and shoulder. What was more, I was full of energy again. I struggled against the bindings with new fiver. On a whim, tested to see if I could summon the earth. The sharp pain still ran through my mark, but it was not quite as sharp as before.

"What was that?" Merlin demanded. I craned my head towards him just in time to see the guard grabbing him with far more force then what was being used with Ember or Cyrus.

"Oh, this?" Nikolai wiggled the empty syringe in the air, "Pure Type W essence. A little injection of this into a water type and it is as if they were never drained at all. Sadly, it does not work on those who have been drained completely."

"But Terra is Type E-" Cyrus began.

"Exactly." The wolfish smile pulled back on Nikolai's lips.

I looked down at the sight of the injection. A patch of skin there was transparent with a rippling surface just like the spot over Merlin's heart. My breath hitched.

Nikolai turned back to me, "And how do you feel Miss Chase?"

If he were any closer I would have gladly spit in his face, "Go to hell!"

"In case you haven't noticed Miss Chase, I am already perpetually burning." Despite my outburst, Nikolai looked absolutely delighted, "No negative effects to a double strain. A new mark. The patient is still quite strong." I could hear the scribbling of notes somewhere near my head. "Now let's try again."

The pod closed around me. I heard more screaming and the familiar hiss of the essence being extracted from my body. It didn't take as long this time before the stars formed in front of my eyes. At that moment, the pod hissed open again.

I groaned as he stood over me.

"Miss Chase..."

"Go to hell."

A long exasperated sigh drained from his lips, "So uncooperative. It could have been so much easier on you." Nikolai prepared another syringe. My eyes were closed when he pressed the needle into my thigh. The site of the injection felt insubstantial. As if it had floated away while the rest of me remained chained to the table. I didn't need to ask what type he had just injected.

With the newest rush of energy, I opened my eyes. "What is the point of all this?" Nikolai tilted his head in curiosity, so I elaborated, "You say you want our cooperation. If you are trying to torture me into submission I'll just save you the time. I would die before I betray the resistance. As would Merlin, Ember, and Cyrus. This is pointless."

At that, Nikolai chuckled. "Oh is that what you think I'm doing?" He laughed again, deeper this time, "No dear girl I am not torturing you. I'm torturing him." Nikolai nodded his head towards Merlin. He leaned over me then, lowering his voice but still loud enough that I knew Merlin, Cyrus, and Ember would hear every word. "You see Miss Chase. I find that people are full of bravado when it is their own wellbeing at stake. As you are showing here. But when it is the wellbeing of a loved one... well... that is a different sort of torment."

My throat tightened. I could only pray that he wouldn't see the panic crawling and edging up my neck. "Merlin wouldn't help you. He knows I would rather die than have him betray anyone."

Nikolai smiled softly, almost pitying. "But would he betray you by letting you die when you could live?"

"Terra don't listen to him!" Merlin's voice sounded thick. I closed my eyes, holding back the sting of tears.

Nikolai patted my shoulder. I found that it was only warm, not burning as I might have expected. The touch disgusted me. "When I am the only thing that stands between you and your death, I think he will be quite willing to do as I command."

A sob caught in my throat as the pod closed yet again. There were no stars this time. I woke to Nikolai slapping me hard across the face. I sputtered though the pull of unconsciousness was close behind me. I heard Nikolai preparing another syringe. There was only one left for him to try at this point. If only I had my powers. I could just skewer him in stone. A needle pressed into my other leg and just as it broke the skin I realized what I needed to do.

Fire was the worst. It burned through my veins and for the first time I couldn't hold back the scream. My body arched against the table. I fell back down in a shaking heap. So that was going to be the worst of it. I could do this. I could keep Nikolai distracted long enough for Merlin's, Ember's, and Cyrus' powers to come back. For us to escape.

"Answer a question for me." I murmured once I had regained the ability to talk once again.

Nikolai leaned over me again. "Yes, Miss Chase?"

I took a breath, summoning the bravado I knew I had stored away somewhere. It was just pain, if that was the worst he could do it wasn't so bad. I already knew what it was to think that I was dying. "Why make Ember and Cyrus watch?" I asked him. "You obviously care about them. But you're willing to hurt them like this?"

Something of tenderness passed the fiery plains of Nikolai's face, "A lesson Miss Chase. I want them to be here when your lover breaks. I want them to see that I am the only one in their lives they can really trust. I, the only one who has never betrayed them."

Cyrus was up out of his seat. It took two of the guards to restrain him this time, "You killed our Mother!" he screamed.

Nikolai raised an eyebrow at his nephew, "Oh is that how Marcus tells the story?" The fire in Nikolai's face darkened, "I wasn't the one who pulled the trigger."

"How are you so sure that Merlin will betray them at all?" I asked.

Nikolai turned back to me, "Because with every new mark, Telluria spreads quicker through your body."

I looked to Merlin, fear in his eyes. I held his gaze as the pod closed again.

CHAPTER FIFTEEN

Out of the Fire

Earth was next. The cool familiarity of my own element was almost a relief. It didn't last long. Nikolai began the cycle of elements again, injecting me with water, then air. When he slapped me awake again, I bit back a whimper knowing what came next. Outside the sky was turning the deep pink of dusk.

As Nikolai prepared the syringe, I locked my gaze with Merlin. He had his hands clasped together so tight his knuckles were white. I saw the wretched look on his face and softly shook my head. I know he wanted to stop it. Nikolai had been right, he was torturing Merlin more than he was torturing me. As the needle pressed into the side of my neck, I mouthed one word, water.

When the fire came, I bit my lip until I tasted blood to stop from screaming. My nails dug into my palms as I silently writhed on the table. Beads of sweat trickled down my brow and despite the newest rush of energy, I felt like I had run a marathon.

Before Nikolai could close the pod again, something tackled him to the ground. Water splashed my face and Merlin was standing over me pulling the bindings free. The moment I was free, Merlin pulled me into his arms and crushed his lips against mine.

"Yeah yeah yeah. Kiss your princess later." Ember had fire in her hands, "Terra I hate to ask but I don't suppose you could take down the window?"

Merlin held me up. I gave a little nod and focused on the window. Nothing. Not a ripple. I didn't feel anything through my mark at all. "I... I must be too weak still. I can't-"

The couch suddenly lifted itself in the air and hurled at the window. It cracked, but it didn't break. "Just as well." Cyrus muttered, "Jumping into the water from this height would be like hitting concrete. And we probably shouldn't trust our powers to catch us just yet." Cyrus led the way towards the door, pushing guards out of the way with a gust of wind. Nikolai was stumbling to his feet near the door.

"If you leave this room I can't protect you," Nikolai pleaded. I could hear the real worry in his voice. "Stay."

"I'm sorry Uncle," Cyrus pushed Nikolai out of the way. "This is my family. After what you did to Mother, and now Terra, you are dead to me."

"Cyrus no-" Nikolai reached but was stopped by a wall of fire. He scoffed, "This girl is nothing! She and her lover will betray you!"

Cyrus and Ember blasted the room with a whirlwind of fire. We ran out of the room and Merlin slammed closed the doors behind us. We didn't really have a plan, we just ran down the way we came. The alarms sounded before we ever got down the first corridor.

"Oh, lovely." Cyrus bit out.

I was struggling to keep up. My legs were lead. Every breath was a labour. Merlin came to an abrupt stop and knelt down in front of me, "Funny it's like the day we met."

There was only time for the briefest nods before I climbed on his back. We were running back in the direction of our cell when we came across corridors that were littered with stone spires.

"Terra did you-" Cyrus looked towards the stone with a question in his eyes.

"It wasn't me."

Our answer came barreling around the corner. Marcus. How in the name of New Atlantis was Marcus here?

"Cyrus! Ember!" Marcus ran up to his children and pulled them into a fierce embrace.

"Father!" Tears of relief were in Ember's eyes, "How did you know where to find us?"

Marcus looked tired and grim. "Josh found out you were captured. I knew Nikolai would never risk the cure on you two." He kissed the top of his daughter's head, "I knew he would bring you straight to him. I could only hope that Terra and Merlin would be here as well. Now come quickly. There's a boat waiting for us in the basement. Arthur's waiting for us on the island."

We started into motion again. Marcus at the helm with his children at his side. Merlin and I lagged a little behind but Merlin was doing well enough keeping up with me on his back. "Where are we?" Merlin asked.

"Azores," Marcus answered simply as he led us to a flight of stairs. "The centre of Nikolai's manufactured utopia."

The stairs were not empty. Earth, air, fire, and water cleaved a path through the pursuing officers until we made it to the bottom.

Just off the steps, we passed a room filled with essence tanks. It must have been the energy supply for the base and the island. The next room was filled with computers. Marcus hesitated for a fraction of a second, visceral hate in his expression.

"Father, we need to go." Cyrus urged forward.

Marcus shook his head as if clearing away his thoughts, "If I only had an hour in that room. The good I could do." He continued forward, a hesitancy clinging to his bones. "That is the heart of the compulsion. Nikolai gives his orders and they are broadcasted to the cured around the world. Someday, we'll come back here." Marcus promised.

Ember paused, looking back at the room. Her hands filled with fire, "Let's destroy it then."

"Ember no!" Marcus put his hand out. "We don't know what will happen if the signal is lost. Maybe nothing. Maybe..." He stopped and shook his head, "Just don't. The risk is too great."

Reluctantly, Ember turned to follow again. Marcus brought us down one last flight of steps and at once I could smell the salt water. We were on the loading dock on the bottom-most level of New Atlantis. From here I could see that the entire complex was held above the ocean on stilts. A small boat waited for us. Looking towards the island, I wondered why Nikolai chose here of all places for his headquarters. Was it just so that he could hide what he had become?

"Marcus..."

We were not alone. Nikolai had somehow beaten us there. He stood at the far edge of the dock with a hulking snake-like machina poised over his shoulder. "Leaving so soon?"

We turned to face him. The man of fire, with a monster of cold hard steel. "I'm afraid we have another engagement, Nikolai." Marcus answered, his voice full of venom, "We will come to visit again soon."

A saddened look crossed Nikolai's expression, "No... I don't think you will."

The machina creaked to life. It uncoiled from around itself and the tail struck out, plucking Cyrus off his feet.

Immediately the cobra-like head was smashed into the ground by a miniature tornado. Ember ran over, drenching the machina in flame so far as to not hit her brother.

"Merlin! Get the boat ready!" Marcus shouted and ran for Nikolai.

I slid off Merlin's back and he helped me into the boat. He untied all but one of the mooring lines, "Will you be alright here alone?" He asked me.

I nodded, "Be careful." I wished I could be of some use as well.

Ember and Cyrus were battling the machina on their own. The head was molten steel and Cyrus had managed to wiggle free of the tail. The structure was a hulking burning mass of metal and gears. The tail swung, pulling the rest of the body along towards Cyrus and Ember. With the combined effort of air and fire, the tail began to melt. The machina was hurled into the back wall of the loading docks. There it remained still.

Nearby, Nikolai and Marcus were locked in hand to hand combat. Marcus was giving all that he had, summoning the earth to rise up against Nikolai. But Nikolai was a Tellurian too. Even without the direct use of his power, the stone melted as fast as it was created. Marcus was slowly finding himself dredging through molten sludge.

"Father!" Cyrus knocked Nikolai back with a gust of wind. Merlin stepped up, keeping Nikolai occupied with turrets of water while Cyrus pulled his father out of the molten stone. Marcus' legs were badly burnt, and Cyrus helped him back to the boat where Ember was now also waiting. "Merlin! It's time to go!" Cyrus called to the only one who remained on the dock.

Just as Merlin was about to turn to follow, a look of inspiration crossed his eyes. He turned, grabbed a metal bar, and hit Nikolai hard over the head. The man of fire fell to the ground out cold. With a rush of water, Merlin half dragged, half slid Nikolai's weight across the dock and into the boat. There he tugged on the last mooring line and used it to tie Nikolai's hands together.

Merlin put his hand in the water and we were pushed by the generated waves towards the shore.

Behind us, the dock was smoking. Small fires were burning and arcs of energy sparked off the machina.

We were free.

Marcus smiled broadly at his children, "You two really did me proud." He then gave Nikolai's body a kick, "Good idea grabbing him Merlin."

Merlin beamed, "Let's just treat him better then he did us hm?" Speaking of, he looked back to me. I was leaning against the side of the boat, "Terra? How are you doing?"

Tears stung my eyes. I didn't want to dampen our victory. "I can't use my powers," I whispered. I had tried multiple times throughout the escape. The earth felt foreign to me.

I saw the desperation in Merlin's face. If I couldn't use them, Telluria would begin to progress again just as Nikolai said.

Cyrus too looked grim. He put a hand on my shoulder, "We'll figure it out. I promise Terra."

I gave a feeble nod and looked back at the building. A plume of smoke was billowing out of the loading dock. The machina's deformed tail made a great sweep. The shattered sound of breaking glass introduced an opalescent gas into the grey smoke.

"Merlin faster!" Marcus screamed and stumbled to the back of the boat as the flames licked the opalescent gas.

The resulting explosion flipped the boat, hurling it towards shore. I tumbled through salt water, my hands scraping for solid ground. My nails broke on clumps of sand and debris. An inferno spiralled around my line of sight through the dark sea.

By sheer reflex, I reached for my element. Something grabbed my wrist and pulled me towards shore.

I crawled, coughing and sputtering onto the sandy beach. A piece of broken seaweed was tied to my wrist. Around me, I hear similar sounds from the others reaching shore. I blinked away the salt and looked around.

Miraculously, we were all there. All lined up on the beach with a knot of seaweed around one limb. Nikolai had a gash in his head, though his chest still rose and fell with breath. Merlin stumbled up beside me, grasping me in his arms. "By God Terra, are you okay?"

Numbly I nodded, holding him so tight I might never let go.

It could have been fine. Everything could have been okay. A wail pierced the silence. Cyrus and Ember were kneeling on either side of Marcus. My heart dropped, and we stumbled over to them.

Marcus was on his back. A sharp gasp escaped my lips when I saw him. He had taken the brunt of the explosion. His entire front was covered in burns with pieces of shrapnel piercing his flesh. Yet, he was smiling. He lifted a hand to Ember's face. "You... are so very much like your mother." His voice was hoarse.

"D-daddy... It'll be okay. We can fix this..." Tears were rolling down her cheeks.

Marcus shook his head, "No... you can't. Ember... take care of Cyrus. Remind him to smile."

Ember nodded, holding her father's hand against her cheek.

Marcus turned his head to Cyrus then. Cyrus' shoulders were shaking with unshed tears. "Cyrus... I know you'll do me proud. Finish our work."

Cyrus touched his father's hand, "I will."

A soft smile pulled at Marcus' lips. He died looking into the faces of his children. When the last breath eased from his body, Cyrus reached over and closed his father's eyes. Ember kissed her father's head.

I buried my face in Merlin's chest and wept. I felt his arms around me, and the sun behind us ebbed closer to the horizon.

#

The flight was silent. Nikolai was tied to a seat. Marcus' body was sleeping in cargo, where Arthur promised, again and again, it would be colder. Part of me wanted to put Nikolai in cargo too.

The only sound that punctuated the silence was Ember's muffled sobs, and Cyrus softly whispering to her. Sometime after midnight, Ember was lulled into the comforting arms of sleep. Only then did I see Cyrus' carefully maintained guise of the strong older brother

185

crack. He allowed only the tiniest gasping sob, and the tears flowed silently down his cheeks until he too succumbed to sleep.

All the while I was curled up in Merlin's arms on the small couch of seats. Neither of us had moved since leaving the island. My legs were going stiff beneath me and I carefully stretched them out.

"You awake?" Merlin's breath of a whisper came from somewhere over my left ear. I had assumed that he too had fallen asleep. Or maybe he was was only so still because he thought I was.

"Yeah," I breathed back and untangled myself from his arms. I could see his face. There was a cut just over his eyebrow. The blood was smeared down the side of his jawline. I wasn't sure he even noticed. His t-shirt, once green, was stained with soot and more blood. His normal smell of salt and seafoam was masked with smoke.

"How?" He looked me over, "You were so tired before..."

I shrugged, "I am tired," I whispered. "Everything aches. But... I don't know... my mind doesn't want to sleep I guess."

"Ter-" The single syllable of my name sounded so broken and aching. "You're not-" He swallowed, "I won't lose you."

My throat tightened. I wanted to cry, to scream, to break down in wailing sobs like I did in that cave behind my house.

Merlin looked down at my hands. On one wrist was my original mark. On the other, was water. I could see my veins just under my skin. "It could be the Water." Merlin brushed his thumb against the underside of my wrist. The touch sent a tingle of sensation across the sensitive flesh.

"What do you mean?" I asked.

"Well..." He raised my wrist and kissed the highways of visible veins and arteries. "When I first got sick, I could never sleep. Even now sometimes, I'll wake up long before the dawn and be wide awake no matter what I try. Water doesn't like to be still."

I shuddered, "but I need in to be still. I need everything to just stop." Tears stung my eyes. My voice had reached a shrill peak and Ember shifted in her sleep. I froze as she settled back down. She and Cyrus looked so peaceful. They deserved that much.

Merlin lifted his hands to cup my face, "Terra..." He kissed my forehead, my eyelids, my lips. "Watching what he did to you without being able to do anything to stop it, it was the hardest hours of my life. I would have gladly drowned him to make it stop. If only I knew killing him would still mean keeping you." He kissed my lips again. Slow and sweet, a thousand unsaid words etched from his lips to mine. "I can fight now. We both can."

My mouth parted. I met his unwavering gaze. I wish I could be as certain as him. Did he feel how every mention of the procedure and my fate sent a shiver down my spine? "Is that why you took him?" I nudged my head in the direction of Nikolai.

Merlin looked sheepish. "While I wish I could say I had the greater good in mind, I'm afraid I'm guilty as charged. My motives were completely selfish and I'm not sorry." His gaze deepened, "he did promise, after all, to keep you alive. While I know you'll never step near a pod again, having him might be useful."

I couldn't help but smile. I wrapped my arms tight around his neck and drew him close.

"Why thank you, Mr Fletcher, for your glowing faith in my skills. I would, of course, be delighted to continue working with your beloved."

My spine stiffened. My veins filled with fire at the sound of Nikolai's voice.

Merlin sat up, half guarding me from Nikolai despite that Nikolai was very firmly tied to the seat. "The tables have turned Nikolai," Merlin hissed. Every muscle in his body was straining. Evidently, he didn't want to risk waking Ember and Cyrus either.

Nikolai sounded merely amused, "so they have." He shifted in the seat as if trying to make himself comfortable. "Or rather, from my point of view things remain the same. Miss Chase is still at my mercy and we are still working towards the same goal."

"I am not at your mercy." I clenched the seat to keep myself from getting up and slapping him.

Nikolai sighed softly. He looked to his niece and nephew curled up asleep and he smiled tenderly. Did he notice their tear-streaked faces? "Give it a week, Miss Chase." He whispered, not looking at me. "A week and you'll be begging me to take you back to my lab."

"There is no lab." The words were out and I felt a brief surging wave of victory at his horrified expression.

"What did you do?" For the first time since meeting him, Nikolai seemed truly unhinged.

Merlin put a protective arm around me, "Your headquarters blew up. Your machina broke the essence tanks while there was a fire on the dock. It's gone, all gone. You lose Nikolai."

Nikolai struggled, panic filling his expression, "The control room! Did that-" We all froze as the siblings stirred again. We held a long tense silence until it was certain they were asleep.

"Everything is gone," I answered. "You should feel blessed you're even alive."

"Do you have any idea what you have done?" Nikolai slumped, dull horror on his face, "We are almost out of time. Soon...soon you will be begging for my help. I only pray that it will not be too late."

CHAPTER SIXTEEN

Fall

The funeral was held in the flower gardens outside the mansion. It was a sunny day. Cyrus and Ember chose to bury their father beneath the oldest oak tree. Several elementalists volunteered to make the marking stone. It was a smooth grey marble with Marcus' name written in onyx. Everyone wore a black band around their arm.

Marcus' casket was made of the same smooth grey marble as the marker. Four wind elementalists, which included Cyrus and Josh, lowered it into the ground. Cyrus led the funeral, speaking about his father's life, about his proudest accomplishments. Ember recounted a favourite memory she had of her father, him teaching her to dance in their old house when she was just a little girl. Others came up and said a few words of remembrance. Little was said of how he died. This was a moment to celebrate Marcus' life.

At the end of it, a line formed with Ember and Cyrus at the front. Cyrus made a small gesture, and a breeze fluttered through the leaves of the oak tree. Ember lifted her hand and a flame no bigger than that of a candle was left hovering in the air. One by one members of the resistance came forward to offer their elemental gifts. Soon more flames filled the air. Water droplets hovered like time stopped rain. Precious stones were placed around the marker. Those who didn't have powers of their own left flowers or some other trinket. When everyone else had turned to leave, Merlin and I stepped forward. Merlin created a robin of water that left his hands and perched atop Marcus' marking stone.

I realized that I had nothing. I let go of Merlin and knelt in front of the marker. "Thank you," I whispered.

I began to get up but paused and touched the ground. For days I had tried to regain control over my powers, assuming I could still use them at all. Stone didn't answer anymore, neither did any of the others. So I simply asked for something, anything. When I pulled my hand away, my breath caught to see a stem of forget-me-nots at the corner of the stone.

I stood and pulled my shawl a little tighter around my shoulders. It was nearly fall and the winds were getting cooler. It was strange to think that the resistance had been my home and family for nearly a year.

Silently, I walked back to Merlin. He was standing with Ember and Cyrus. Tears sparkled in Ember's eyes. "Thank you for being here." She said softly.

I smiled gently, "The med bay saw no reason to keep me there any longer."

"Will you be alright?" Cyrus asked, and his eyes flicked for just a second to some of my visible marks. The scorch of fire on my neck was the hardest to keep covered.

I bit my lip and glanced back at the marker stone. "I... don't know." I didn't know what else to say. "I'm not giving up just yet." I thought of the flower on the grave. Maybe...

"So..." Merlin put his arm around me. We had already talked about the marks, how they were growing little by little. We agreed not to let it rule our every moment. "What now?" There was a light hope in his voice.

Cyrus ran a hand through his hair, "With Nikolai in custody and the headquarters destroyed, New Atlantis is struggling. Seems they can't cure anyone because the programming doesn't work anymore. They are lucky they are still keeping up with the ration deliveries or else it might be the return of the riots."

I sunk deeper into Merlin's arms, "Has there been any news on the cured? The compulsion hasn't been affected has it?"

Cyrus shook his head, "I haven't heard anything strange. The hope is that they'll just continue on with whatever programming they have." Cyrus' hand twitched into a fist for just a second, "Nikolai is still waiting for the worst, however."

A bitter edge ground on Cyrus' voice. Despite his age, he was elected the new leader of the resistance. People trusted him. He worked closely with his father for as long as the resistance had been in operation. For most, Cyrus was the obvious choice.

"Did you want to go inside?" Merlin wrapped both arms around me as he spoke to Cyrus and Ember, "They made all of Marcus' favourites for lunch."

Ember shook her head. "I'm not hungry." There was a bench in the garden not far from the oak tree. She went to sit down. "I think I'll stay with Father just a little longer."

Pulling away from Merlin, I took the spot next to her and put an arm over her shoulders. Around us, the elements twinkled in the afternoon sun.

#

Several days later I went to visit Nikolai. I was alone. Cyrus was busy trying to figure out our next move with much help from Josh. Ember had thrown herself into the maintenance of Arthur's plane. And Merlin... I wasn't sure where Merlin was exactly. He had some work to do after breakfast and I pretended I had a checkup with the med bay. I didn't want him to know where I was going.

Nikolai was being kept in a carbon lined cell that he wouldn't easily be able to melt. Not that he would try. Even now he refused to use his powers and insisted on using Marcus' pod to drain off the excess essence. The fact that he was now single-handedly powering the base didn't seem to bother him.

When I got there, Kalle was guarding the door. He was sitting in a chair with a book in his lap.

191

"Kalle? Would it be alright if I spoke to Nikolai for a moment?"

He gave me a cautious look. The story of what Nikolai had done to me had spread through the base like wildfire. Most people assumed I was living on borrowed time. "Are you sure Terra?"

I nodded, already having worked up the nerve just to come down here.

"Alright then." Kalle stood and slid his book under his arm. "I'll just be down the hall little ways. Scream if you need me okay?"

I nodded again. Kalle walked down the hall and around the corner out of sight. I had a feeling he would still be able to hear everything, but at least he was giving the illusion of privacy.

"To what do I owe the honour, Miss Chase?" Nikolai's voice was calm and silky. I looked through the bars of his door. He too was reading. Slowly he closed his book and set it down on the cot. The single piece of furniture he had. Better accommodations then he gave Merlin and me in fact.

I stood in front of the bars. "New Atlantis is crumbling without you. Resistances around the world have been taking down the clinics, releasing the sick."

He raised an eyebrow at me, "How kind of you to bring me the news but I am afraid my nephew had been keeping me quite up to date." Nikolai laced his fingers together on his lap, "But that is not why you are here is it Miss Chase?"

I swallowed hard, "I want to know what you did to me."

A trickling laugh escaped his lips, "I think you know. If I remember correctly, you were there, and awake. Most of the time anyway."

Without meaning to, I slammed my hand against the bars, "That's not what I meant! I can't use my powers anymore. I can't control stone or any of the other elements. The marks are growing..."

"And as a last resort, you come to me?" The irony was not beyond him, "And here I thought you didn't like my brand of cure."

I ground my teeth, "That's not what I meant and you know it." My voice was little more than a hiss. Not wanting to lose myself, I took a step back and sucked in a breath.

Something caught Nikolai's attention. Wide eyes, he got up and moved to the bars. I recoiled when he reached for my arm, "Miss Chase... have you... experienced anything peculiar? Since the procedure? Plants or, even animals reacting to you?"

I backed up as far as I could, pushing my back against the wall. I could feel the blood draining from my face. The forget-me-not. Perhaps even the seaweed that I remembered pulling me out of the water.

"You have!" Nikolai clapped his hands together, "I've done it! I've really done it. After all this time-"

"What have you done?" My demanding tone brought him back to the present, though did not dampen his spirits in the slightest.

"You are my Vita! The purest and perfect of the elements. In you, I have created the catalyst for Gaia's cure. The element of life."

#

I asked Cyrus, Ember, and Merlin to meet me in the solarium after supper. I went there after seeing Nikolai, my mind whirling from what he had told me. I didn't want to believe it was true but how could I not? In desperation, I tested his theory. I knew what element to pull for now. I approached the rows of herbs and flowers and stroked the unopened pod of a lily. At once the pod opened, the red and white petals reaching not towards the sun, but to me.

I sat curled on the wicker settee when the others arrived. Merlin took one look at my face and pulled me into his arms. "What happened?"

"I went to see Nikolai."

His arms tightened around me, "Did he hurt you?"

I buried my face in his chest. I could feel the sting of tears in my eyes. "He told me what I am," I whispered, my voice muffled against Merlin's shirt. "He thinks he can use me to cure the planet, and therefore, everyone."

"Terra." Cyrus spoke somewhere over Merlin's shoulder, "He can't hurt you anymore. We won't let him."

Silently I shook my head, "The damage has already been done."

I pulled out of Merlin's arms and went back to the window boxes. Merlin followed, slipping his arm around my waist. Cyrus and Ember were just behind me as I reached for a patch of chamomile. The flowers grew taller, the unopened pods sprang with a wash of tiny white petals. I heard Ember suck in a gasp.

"He called it Vita. The element of life."

Cyrus' mouth pressed into a hard line. That expression always reminded me so much of Marcus. "I'll look through Father's notes. Maybe he mentioned something about it." He paused then, the light filtering in his eyes, "You do know what this means though right?"

The corners of my mouth tugged as I looked down at my original mark on my arm. "I'm not going to die." Already there were signs of the mark receding again.

Ember giggled and pulled me from Merlin so that she could hug me. "I knew you wouldn't! You're too stubborn to let something like a power trouble stop you." She kissed both my cheeks before releasing me.

When I looked up at Merlin again, his own expression was that of aching sweet relief. He tugged on my hand, drawing me close before threading both hands in my hair. I couldn't help but grin as he brought his lips to mine in such a kiss that I was soon breathless and dizzy.

"I love you, Terra." He breathed against my skin.

I pulled away slightly, looking up into his blue-grey eyes of the sky after a storm. "And I you."

We remained in the solarium as the orange light of the setting sun streamed through the windows. "So what now?" I asked, still cradled in Merlin's arms. "New Atlantis has fallen, more or less. At least they've stopped curing people."

Cyrus sighed and gave a little shrug, "For the time being, keep spreading the word that there is another way. It should be easier now. And research this 'cure' that Nikolai is on about."

Merlin created a tiny water bird to fly around the room. It landed on Cyrus' shoulder with a splash. "Healing the earth. Sure, no problem at all."

Despite the sarcasm, I heard the hope in his voice. A world without Telluria, I couldn't even remember such a time.

"A bit of penicillin and a vita kick start and it'll be good as new." I kissed Merlin's cheek, wishing that it really would be that simple.

EPILOGUE

The late summer sun shone down on the New York City centre. Once it had been in Times Square, but a series of unfortunate events left the area destroyed beyond foreseeable repair. Now the centre was in Central Park where market stalls and shoppers trampled the too tall grass of the Great Lawn. A few old men sat in the shade of the trees at the edge of the lawn, reminiscing of the days of their youth when New York City was a spectacle of wealth and theatre.

Near them, a platform was set up as a makeshift stage. No one was ever hired as a professional performer but every so often someone would brave the stage and entertain the masses with their talents. If they were good, often the performer would receive gifts of food, supplies or little trinkets that were of no particular use but held some intrinsic value.

On that day, a woman climbed on the stage. She was small and plain wearing a blue dress and long dark hair coiled up in plaits. She stood in the very centre of the stage and began to sing an aria that had been taught to her by her grandmother. Her hands poised in the air, moving like birds with the ebb and flow of the notes. It was beautiful. A small crowd gathered around her, tears filling the eyes of many who watched.

A restlessness settled on the audience as the aria reached its crescendo. What moments ago was considered beautiful was slowly being considered as little more than squawking. The woman was a bird making far too much noise in a den of foxes.

Furtive glances moved between the people. Those who had the faded marks of the healed all had the same look in their eyes; hatred, danger, the feral urge to rip and render. Lips pulled back against snarling teeth and a thousand murderous smiles glinted towards the singing woman.

Acknowledgements

First I would like to thank my husband Jeremy Trask for all the support he gave me throughout writing Telluria. Thanks for being the person I bounced a thousand questions off of, and understanding when my brain was still stuck in the story I was trying to write. Love you to the moon and back.

Thanks to my parents and parents-in-law, Gloria, Jody, Darin, Linda, and Jerry. Thank you for letting my imagination soar, and giving me the opportunity to follow this dream.

Many thanks to my beta readers including Charlotte, Gloria (Mom), Linda (Mom-in-law), and my sisters Madison and Chloe. Special thanks to Charlotte who helped so much with the editing and with the London chapters.

Now it's time for the weirder, though still important acknowledgements. Thanks to Disturbed for your song "Another Way To Die", which I have long since declared the unofficial theme song of this book. Thanks to Google Earth for letting me go places I've never been and digitally walk in the shoes of my characters. Lastly, thanks to James Lovelock for your Gaia Hypothesis.

And of course, thanks to you, yes you, reading this now. Hope you liked it!

About the Author

Jodi Trask currently resides in Newfoundland, Canada with her husband Jeremy Trask. She has always had a love for stories and has been writing from a young age.

Before writing Telluria, Jodi studied at Memorial University of Newfoundland - Grenfell Campus and earned a degree in Environmental Biology.